D1488369

The Cailleach of Sligo

About the Author

Michael B. Roberts is an anthropologist and storyteller, and founder of the Sligo Myths and Legends Summer School (see www. lughzone.com.) He lives in Knock na Hur, County Sligo.

THE CAILLEACH OF SLIGO

Stories and Myths from the Northwest of Ireland

Michael B. Roberts

Illustrations by Conor Gallagher

The Liffey Press

Published by
The Liffey Press
Ashbrook House, 10 Main Street
Raheny, Dublin 5, Ireland
www.theliffeypress.com

A catalogue record of this book is
available from the British Library.

ISBN 978-1-905785-82-7

Printed in the Republic of Ireland by Colour Books

CONTENTS

PREFACE

Stories for Children of All Ages

The stories in this collection were first told when the world was still young. They were intended to explain how the world came into being and how it changed to being merely human. I heard them first as a boy from family, friends, teachers and others. They have been gathered and embellished over the course of my life. I retained them as small fragments of memory that I have tried to reassemble here. I hope you like them. For me they still taste of the long ago, of youth and innocence and of happy times before the world lost its sense of fun and wonder.

Although some of the stories are very old, I have tried to tell them in a new voice. Some are the reflections of a small boy backed up by a lot of reading and experience at a later time. All have truth and wisdom hidden between the lines. You may find your own truth and wisdom in these stories, but all truths are valid.

The stories are generally of the north west of Ireland, or a local version of well known Irish tales, but they reflect myths and legends that can be found around the globe. All have an Irish content but a universal theme. Let me know if you have heard other versions of these stories. I love hearing a new variation of a story I already know, or even better a story I haven't heard before.

The children of this world are wiser in their own generation than the children of light.

Beir bua is beannacht.

June 2010
Michael Roberts
'Maigh Tuireadh'
Knock na Hur
County Sligo

INTRODUCTION

Ireland has a long tradition of storytelling. Telling stories is the oldest form of didactic activity and has roots in many cultures. In earliest times the Irish people, in their 'years of wisdom', the time beyond child-bearing for women and beyond hunting for men, had the task of rearing and educating the children. They had the wisdom of experience. The younger adults, those above the age of puberty, were too busy hunting, gathering, herding animals, preparing and cooking food and fending off marauding bears and wolves. All these activities were the domain of the hunters and gatherers and included all the demands the world makes on people to make it difficult to spend much time with very young children.

Women were warriors in the military sense, but also because they spilled their own blood in bringing their children into the world. When the population density increased men and some women changed from being hunters of meat and seafood and became the warriors that defended the local resources of their clan or hearth.

In the years of wisdom, after the child-bearing years, men and women became godparents to the children of their hearth and the providers of remedies for ailments of the body. Some became the organisers of ritual and ceremony designed to heal the mind and the community of their clan of any disturbance that life could bring. Younger people, those who became disabled in the hunt or in battle, could become the healers of the soul in their community, closely coupling ideas of soul or spirit with ideas of community. These groups of wise people were teachers and judges in their community, bringing wisdom to bear on the trials of life.

Teaching children about life was a part of the creation and preservation of the culture for the next generation in particular. People learned from the experiences of living a life and dying a death. They were also philosophical about things that experience did not clarify for them. Ritual and ceremony were designed to supplement the experience of the everyday and the extraordinary. Insights gained by one generation were stored in the form of narrative discourse that we recognise as myth and legend in our generation. Myth explained the mystery of mind and spirit, while legend told the unauthored history of a people. Narratives were handed on, '*ó ghlúin go glúin*', learned at the knee of godparents and grandparents, the wise people.

In earliest times, when population densities were low, the care and well-being of women and children were the primary concerns of the clan. Without children the clan could not survive and continue. Initially, these communities were matri-centred. Women were the main providers of food; they gathered fruits, herbs and root crops, 80 per cent of provisions. Hunting provided the other 20 per cent but, when hunting far from home, hunters had to leave local supplies to the women, children and those in the years of wisdom. Later, when defence became a primary concern, a society based on patriarchy developed with the greatest warrior claiming power and privilege. Few groups remained matri-centered or became matriarchic.

The main controversy for the early people to resolve was the choice between wisdom and war as means of settling disputes. As we will see, many stories explore and examine this major issue. Either they demonstrate the common sense of the wise people or the foolishness of the warriors. Warriors and druids fought battles on different levels and on the grand and the small scale. The stories are full of their insight.

Many of the characters in the stories are reflections of the climate and forces of nature at work in the environment. They also reflect our emotional nature and how our passions and feelings can rule our life. The didactic messages were promoted by the presence in the landscape of the many ancient monuments and megaliths of earliest times.

Growing up in Sligo we were totally surrounded by this ancient landscape and yet most people were hardly conscious of it. Each ancient site had a story attached and some of these stories are included in this book. They have an underlying belief or value system that informed us and formed the very foundations of the thinking of our people.

My later reading told me that our stories had been diminished by time and later cultural influences. They were less rich because of this. Here I hope to retrieve some of that richness. If I have succeeded to some small degree I will be happy.

The 'Cailleach' informs us of the forces at play in our lives that we have little or no control of. At best we can come to terms with them but we cannot conquer them. But who was the Cailleach, and who were the people who created her in the first place? Where did they come from and who told the stories, and why? Questions, questions, so many questions!

This small book is intended to address at least some of these questions. All answers are inadequate, but let me try. And be warned: the stories may raise more questions than they answer.

Dedicated to Irish Storytellers Everywhere

1

THE CAILLEACH OF SLIGO

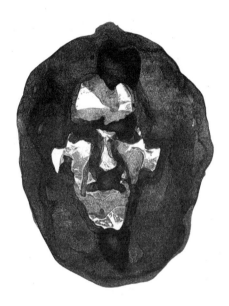

The Cailleach decided to build herself a new house. She liked the view from that new mountain near the sea. She had left that mountain behind, at the far end of it, the time she made the valley of the Shelly Place. That long and rather narrow valley was greening up nicely and the sandy and shelly shore was a pleasant place to walk when her brother Aengus was settling into the sea in the far west. She had made the valley so that she had an unrestricted view from the east side to watch him as he passed each day. He needed watching.

Sometimes he would hide behind the clouds for a long time and the valley would freeze up killing all in her creation. At other times he would get very stimulated and, in a blaze of excitement, the valley would be burned to a crisp where no creature or plant could live. He had done these things before and he needed watching to prevent him from doing it again. Men! No self-control.

The valley was known as Slí na gCaillaig, the way of the Cailleach. She had used a big block of ice to push the mountain of silt into the sea. It had gathered in the estuary of the great river that flowed from the heart of the continent behind her. Some lumps of limestone looked so pretty that she avoided them and when her bull-dozing work was done they looked very well on the horizon of the new landscape. She liked one hill so much, Dartry, that she built herself a house on top of it. It gave her a panoramic view of her new valley that was surrounded by mountains and low hills.

The hard rocks to the south and east had boiled up when the Earth was shifting its sitting position. They were not so easy to move. She managed to knock some big lumps off the top and sides but the main body would not shift. Being a man it was too stubborn to move even when pushed. It dug in its heels and stayed put. Smart woman that she was she just gathered up the loose boulders into her apron and used them to make her home above the rapid waters in the middle of the valley. Nice place to plant some oak trees but that would have to wait.

The boulders left over after her house building project would make another nice summer house by the sea on the other limestone lump she had left there. While flying above the valley, her apron full to breaking point, she became distracted by Aengus. He was making rivers all over the valley and she liked what he was doing.

Suddenly her apron could take the strain no longer. It split and dropped the boulders strewing them all over the west end of the valley. Annoyed, she began to gather them up again until she noticed that it was getting dark. Aengus was nearly asleep. The rocks could wait until morning or maybe even a little longer. That didn't happen.

She was distracted and led astray when she went to bring her cow home before dark. The cow was full of milk and was agitated and impatient to be milked. It was skittish and frisky. As they came around the limestone hill at the east end of the valley, the cow bolted. The Cailleach had started building an underground storehouse in the side of the hill, later called Keash, and had left the doors open when she went about her work of clearing the valley.

The frisky cow, quick as a wink, headed into the mouth of the cave and charged into the black dark of the cave. The Cailleach gave chase and managed to catch the tail of her cow, the *bó buí,* but it was too late. The cow was up to speed and on the tear into the bowels of the earth. The Cailleach held on tight, her arms almost pulled from their sockets, but she held on all night.

Ready to fall down with exhaustion she galloped behind the *bó buí* until it emerged again into the light of day. The Cailleach tumbled and blinked herself back to reality as fast as she could. Luckily enough, she knew where she was. It was where she had been building underground storage ponds all over the midlands to hold the water leaking from the newly made bogs of Ireland. She had no name for it yet, but the later people called it Crúacháin, where the chieftains of Connaght had their yearly hosting. It was a while before she got back to the Sligo again.

The rocks waited for the Cailleach to return next morning but she didn't arrive back to do the job. They waited for a long time, 320 million years in all, until the new people who came to live in the valley finished the job for her of building the house on top of Knock na Rae, the Hill of the Moon.

When she did get back she had her two sisters with her. They were a strange crew with only one eye between the whole lot of them. Of course, they were much older by then, but they were not so busy as the new people had taken on the job of taking care of the land and its smaller features. The Cailleach and her sisters moved underground at Keash, out of sight of the people. They came only to the door after that time, never coming into the full light of day again.

One day, while near the door of the biggest cave at Keash, they heard the cries of a hunting party chasing a stag around the bottom of the hill. The stag, a wily creature, made them work very hard to keep up with him by running up the hill and then down the other side. The men, a group of the Fianna, a group dedicated to protecting the land and its people, were just about to fall down, their legs wobbling from the unending run. The three sisters decided not only that the stag would make a fine meal to fill the pot, but that the Fianna would add a nice flavour also.

To attract them into the cave, on their way to the cooking pot that was steaming on the fire, the three sisters shape-changed into three beautiful young women. They smiled and waved at the passing hunters, covering their face in apparent embarrassment but really to cover the fact that they had only one eye. They had fought so much with each other over the years that they were badly deformed and damaged in their true form.

Fionn, the leader of the Fianna, stopped and the others skidded to a halt behind him. The three sisters smiled. The Fianna smiled and then fell for the bait. They moved up the hill to meet the three women. Men! How easy to catch them out. That is, all except Goll Mac Morna, Fionn's second in command. He got the name Goll not only from the tears that flowed down his face non-stop, but from the fact that he had a leaky bladder. It was an ongoing torment to him. And his bladder was giving him trouble again. All that running up and down hills and not a chance to settle anywhere all morning! Now, when there was some fun in the offing, his bladder made demands on him again. How unfair.

Goll took off around behind the hill of Keash while the Fianna were being escorted into the depths of the cave. Goll felt cheated. He was grumbling and grouching as he went about his unintended business. By the time he had finished and returned to the cave things had changed, radically. The three gorgeous girls were gone and the three ugly sisters had returned. The Fianna were hanging from the roof of the cave above the big steaming pot. They had all their clothes removed and were wrapped in a spider web and left to dangle like dolls until the three sisters were ready to share them out, in three equal portions. And that was what delayed them. The three could not agree who would get which of the Fianna. Being warriors there was not a plump one among them. They were a tough, muscular, sinewy lot. What would be left of them after a bit of a boiling?

Goll took in the scene in a flash. He saw that the sister with the eye in her head was nearest to him. One quick swing of his axe and she had neither eye nor head to work with. The two other sisters came to a quick end also and, in jig time, followed her into the big pot. Their cackles stopped in a flurry of bubbles and steam. The Fianna, looking down from their precarious positions, gave a muffled sigh of relief. Good old Goll. He would be a favourite for a long time after with a lot less teasing about the problem with his waterworks. Goll and his little problem had saved the day, and their necks. Sometimes a little problem can be of great advantage.

On Further Reflection

Maybe now we can think about the answers that these stories offer and, indeed, the real questions being asked. First, let's look at the Cailleach herself. She is the tough side of Mother Nature that brings change. She is the alter ego to the kindly *tSean-mháthair* or *bean feasa*, a grandmother who takes care of small children. She is an icon of winter, that force of nature that shaped the world and still changes the world, often in drastic ways. Recent volcanoes, tsunamis and earthquakes show the Cailleach in action abroad. In recent centuries, thankfully, in Ireland she shows in less drastic ways: flooding, sudden waves on the beach, landslides and rock falls.

In this narrative the Cailleach represents the ice-sheet, the roaring underground torrent and the distraction of men drawing them to their doom when they should be hunting for the needs of their hearths. In Ireland she was at the height of her power during the last ice age between 10,000 and 15,000 years ago. The geography of Sligo was laid during that period.

The Cailleach has many sisters and the old saying is that 'misfortune comes in threes', one shortly after the other. They have one eye between them as we tend to see them one at a time, perhaps one initiated by another.

The Hill of Keash is a prominent flat-topped hill south east of Sligo Town. The story explains how the stones used to build the monuments at Carrowmore and the Maebh's carn on Knock na Rae were delivered to those sites. How else could the

7

boulders have come all the way there without some giant or powerful creature to bring them? These boulders are hard igneous granite stones, not native to the limestone of the Carrowmore area. They came from the Ox Mountains on the opposite side of County Sligo. They were transported in the Cailleach's apron, the sheet of ice that carried them and, in splitting or melting, dropped at Carrowmore. No human effort could have done this. Only a great force of nature could do it and that is who the Cailleach was: a great force of nature, one of a family of natural forces that made the world. Perhaps Goll, with his little waterworks problem, was the force that made the underground tunnel from Keash to Crúacháin. Was this what he was doing behind the mountain?

Some landscape features are natural, constructed by nature. The underground track followed by the *bó buí* and Cailleach actually does exist. It is a cave washed out by underground melt water. The other end of the cave, where it emerges at Crúacháin, is known as the Gates of Hell according to local story. From it have come herds of red and white pigs and dogs that devastated the West of Ireland in the long ago, when God was just a boy.

The name, Keash, sometimes called Keash Corrán, has multiple translations: the young pig, related to Gulbáin; harp, relating to stringed instruments used by the Druids or shamans; and hive because the caves are like a hive of storerooms under the mountain. Keash may also relate to *kish* or *kishean*, translating as basket, which fish were trapped in. Did the fish make it up this far?

Corrán can mean the starting point, where the Cailleach began her push of the ice-block towards the sea; bees, associated with the hive in Keash; and tide, related possibly with the tide of ice that filled the valley or the tide of water that flowed from the valley when the ice melted. There is a sweet-water well at the side of Keash and this too is a possible translation.

Some landscape features, like Méasgáin Maebh, Maebh's 'lump of butter', were constructed by people to honour the Cailleach's sister, Brí, the Great Earth Mother and mother of Brigit. It was made with 103 granite kerb-stones, each weighing between 5 and 10 tons taken from the valley floor to the top of the mountain. Who can say how this was done. The fill material of the great carn, all 50,000 tons of limestone, was mined from the mountain close to where the carn stands in view of all of the people of Sligo today. Maebh resides there now, a later edition of Brí and a name brought by a later people.

The Mother and her daughters were imagined by the early people of the locality who used the stories to explain what was otherwise inexplicable to them. The stories explained such things to me as a child before the science of geology was understandable by me. I hope you like the story. Why not tell it to your children. It will make them curious and help them to feel the awe that nature inspires in us all if we are open to it.

The Cailleach was the first formidable woman I ever met. Since then I have met a few more but she, the Cailleach, was the template or icon for them all. She was small and old and wrinkled, but she was also full of energy and hyperactive. She never stopped moving. There were several short stories about her. Her ubiquitous presence began in those stories but later leaked into the real world in the form of local women who ruled my childhood world. Although these women did not fit the stereotype of the Cailleach, they had enough of her characteristics to make her alive and well, and living in the Sligo of my childhood.

I can still see her in my mind's eye. She looks like a thunder cloud rolling across the valley of Sligo. Her sharp-featured face is etched in the cloud by a bolt of lightening. She sits on her broom, with the Hill of Keash at her back, the Plain of Carrowmore beneath her and Knock na Rae in front of her. She sails on the wind that comes off the ocean. Can you see her?

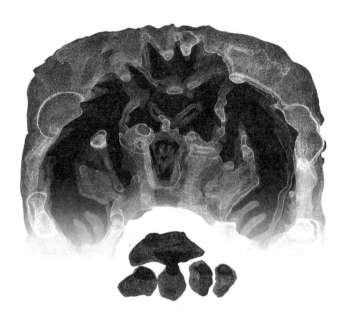

2

Lough Gill: The Lake of Tears

County Sligo is in the northwest of Ireland. All of county Sligo was, in ancient times, covered by the sea so that, even high up in the mountains, shells are still found in abundance. Sligo gets its name from its Irish name of *Sligeagh*, which means 'the Shelly Place'. This name originates from the kitchen middens, a series of ancient domestic dumps filled with cockle, mussel and oyster shells, found in abundance along the foreshore of Sligo's many headlands. One such midden contains over 200,000 tons of discarded shells. There are many such middens.

The early people did not live on the seashore near the middens but took food from the sea and carried it home to the banks of the river that runs from Lough Gill to the sea at Strandhill and Rosses Point. The lake, river and sea characterised Sligo and gave it its shape and a trajectory for its history. The lake on the west side of the town is surrounded by mountains, guardians of the area who stand to attention while gathering water to fill up the lake of Lough Gill. But it was not always a lake. Originally, the old community of the Shelly Place filled the bottom of this valley before it flooded. That was a long time ago, a time of when the local people tell an old story of the creation of the world and Sligo as we know it today. Who were these people? Where did they come from and how did the flood occur? Let me tell you.

Aodh Mór, the chieftain of the Shelly Place, was elected many times to take care of his people. He and his extended family lived in a large safe and dry camp, Dun Aodh, near Slish Wood under Dartry, a mountain famous for it herds of deer and wild goats. The sea, and the attendant threat of raiding parties, was a morning's hike down the valley to the west. Gealla was one of Aodh Mór's many daughters. She spent all of her time walking in the woods, among the flowers and trees that surround Dun Aodh, the great rock that gave elevation and protection to the camp. This rock is better known, at present, as Dooney, a garbled form of Dún Aodh.

Gealla was greatly admired and courted for her beauty and gentle nature and the brightness of her eye. She was popular with the people of the nearby village of Sligo where she often went to search for the crafted goods that the area was famous for. If you wanted to know anything about flowers, trees or the herbs of the area, Gealla was the person to ask. She formed a school to spread her gathered wisdom to others, for the good of her people and the conservation of the many plants that had won her heart.

But the vegetation had competitors for her heart. Many of the local minor chieftains wanted her as a bride. Whoever married Gealla would gain a lot of prestige and influence associated with her family as well as a beautiful wife. Aodh Mór facilitated as many as was seemly to visit his home, hoping to meet his daughter, but to no advantage. Knowledge was at her heart and so was a young man, Oghamra, who lived in the nearby hill on the other side of the lake. Gealla wanted to marry Oghamra, a young and scholarly man who matched her in humour and love of nature. Although a gifted scholar he could not compete with the chieftains for power and influence. Scholars had given way to soldiers a long time ago when the defence of resources became a prime concern. Now that so much was known about the use of resources they, and this knowledge, were taken for granted. Familiarity lessens value.

And there was another problem. Romera was a soldier, old and hardened by battle but wise in the ways of the world. This established and powerful man was arrogant and insensitive and could see no good reason why he should not have Gealla. She would enhance his chances of progress in the pecking order among the chieftains of the region and determine who would replace the aging Aodh Mór when that time came. Gealla's blood-line, obvious beauty and reputation for intelligence and learning would add greatly to his prestige and possibly appear to temper his rough manner and reputation for violence. He gave no thought to what she might want or what might make her happy. For Romera that was not relevant.

He spoke to Gealla's father and made his case for her hand. Aodh Mór was reluctant to even consider this proposition but protocol demanded that he should put it to Gealla. When Gealla was consulted she refused even to consider the proposal because of her love for Oghamra and the repugnant character of Romera. This made Romera very angry and jealous. He was accustomed to having his own way and this rebuff rankled. A mere schoolboy was preferred to a man of his standing and achievements in battle? He looked on Oghamra, his rival for Gealla's hand in marriage, as a mere temporary nuisance. He planned to eliminate this nuisance by fair means or foul. He was not a patient man but he waited for an opportunity to bring change to these circumstances. He did not have long to wait.

One morning, when the day and the moon were new, Oghamra was hiking in the hills to the south of Aodh Mór's camp. He had been sketching the birds of the forest, counting their coloured eggs and collecting feathers from their nests. He could hear someone singing somewhere away in the distance. It was coming from the direction of the cliff, one of his favourite haunts for hawks and eagles, his favourite birds. It was the unmistakable voice of Gealla, of that he was sure. He hummed with delight as he pushed his way silently through the hazel wood until she came into view. She gave the impression that

she was oblivious of his presence while at the same time expecting his arrival. She had spring flowers in her hair and was busily collecting herbs and roots for her medicine potions. She sang with the birds and smiled with the joy of knowing that all was well with her world.

Gealla looked up and smiled softly when Oghamra made his presence known by accompanying her singing with a birdsong. For Oghamra the birds and bees were forgotten for the moment. It felt good to be in Gealla's presence again. He stopped humming and moved closer. He didn't have an opportunity like this very often to talk to her and spend a little time in her company alone. Her attendants were usually at hand but now, carelessly or perhaps not, they had wandered away in search of myrtle that grew in the area. He gaped when he saw her and she smiled quietly at him. He felt a little shy and hesitated to start a conversation. She laughed at his shyness and he grinned at her openness and obvious joy of life. It was one of those all too fleeting, magical moments.

Before any conversation could begin Romera came bursting from the heathers, sword in hand, spluttering with rage and jealousy, with murder on his mind. He had been informed by his spies that Gealla was gathering herbs near the cliff and he meant to discuss his plans and move quickly past the nonsense posed by Oghamra. He wanted to talk to her alone, to persuade her of his burning ardour for her and all the advantages of their coupling. That was now spoiled by the appearance of Oghamra. He could see now that his opportunity for negotiation was gone and his anger flared. It knew no bounds. He charged like a wild boar in a blind, black rage. In a moment it was all over. Oghamra lay mortally wounded, his life's blood flowing into the soft mosses at the foot of the cliff, the look of surprise left permanently registered on his face.

Gealla was in shock, astonished at the speed of change in the order of her life. She held Oghamra's head in her lap, scattering the herbs and seeds she had collected earlier when the day was young. Her feeling of tragedy rose to a crescendo as she sobbed and wailed her grief and screamed for help. The gentle young man she had hoped to spend her life with lay dying in her arms. His eyes were wide open but then slowly closed, never to open again. Gealla's final cry of anguish called everybody within hearing distance to her aid. All who heard it knew immediately that something awful had just happened.

Romera stood in the horror of his own actions. He realised in a flash that he had just killed off any hope he might ever have had of finding favour with Gealla. His mind was overwhelmed with the horror of what he had done. He had just destroyed his own life as well as that of the young couple on the ground in front of him. He ran from the scene knowing only dread, darkness and despair. His head-long flight took him to the deepest hollow of the nearby valley, in a wild search for some place to hide from his own people, from his tragic de-nouement, from himself and the stench of his own foulness. All his plans and schemes were suddenly in ruin. There, in deep despair and anguish, he ended his own earthly life, falling on his sword he opened his belly to the earth. He raced into the Otherworld searching for relief from this open wound in his soul. Would he ever find it?

Later that morning, Gealla was found by her distraught handmaidens, lying dead across the head of Oghamra. She had died of sorrow, her heart broken, her story in fragments and her life ended. Her flowing tears gathered in a pool at the foot of the cliff. This well of tears and sorrow had overflowed and tumbled down into the valley where Romera lay in a red pool of blood and despair. The tears of her handmaidens and all the people of Dún Aodh joined in Gealla's stream, overflowed the deepening pools of grief, filling the valley of Sligo and forming the lake we see today.

Aodh Mór could not speak for a long time afterwards. He arranged to have the maiden of the Shelly Place, her body cov-ered in her favourite flowers and herbs, floated down the stream of tears and out on to the new lake. All the warriors of the district, great mountains of men, stood to attention around the lake, the lake of Gealla's and her people's tears. In time the birds came to nest on this small, floating island, to sing to their young friend and hatch their eggs in the keeping of her lap. They brought her gifts of twigs and heathers, grasses and flow-ers and, in time, the island took hold in the lake. With the pass-ing of the years the island became as beautiful as the young woman who began its construction that bright spring morning, gathering flowers and herbs at the cliff above her home.

Oghamra's and Romera's bodies were carried to the top of the nearby hills and were covered with stones, monuments to the foolishness and sadness of this world and reminders that the Otherworld is all around us, ready to break through in a moment of love or joy, anger or jealously. Lough Gill, the lake of Gealla, flooded and covered over the village of Sligeach forcing its people to move further downstream to where the river runs into the sea. Aodh's Mór's camp was abandoned when he died. There was too much sorrow in that one place.

The experience of such tragedies gathers in the estuary of life to form the wisdom of the ages. Such stories are never forgotten. Still, the people of the Shelly Place visit the well at the cliff, Tober an Ailt, to consider the story of Gealla, Oghamra and Romera and how they met their sad fate. In this way wisdom is accumulated and made available to later generations.

Is brónach an scéal é.
[What a sad story.]

On Further Reflection

This story has a lot to tell us. Like so many stories in our tradition it features a young girl, a young and gentle man and an older and tougher warrior. The older man represents the setting Sun, the end-time of a unique period when great change arrives. The younger man represents the rising Sun that displaces the setting Sun while the young girl represents the Moon. The story tells us that change is in the nature of things; that innocence is made rough and love can have tragedy attached. The carns are constant reminders of such change. They represent the soul or character in the stories and were put in place to remind us of the attached message.

Emotions and feeling tend to determine much of what we do. Warriors can represent the passionate or emotional side of us, while the scholar can represent our reasoning and reasonable side. The battle between these two aspects of being human rages constantly. So many early battles were set between Connaght as the place of wisdom and autumn and Ulster as the place of war and winter. The stories represent this ongoing and often tragic dilemma when we lose our most beautiful and best to our worst side when we go to war, walking away from a more reasoned outcome of our disputes.

Romera was a warrior. He did what he had been prepared to do: he attacked Oghamra and then he attacked himself. Oghamra was a scholar in preparation for becoming a *saoi*, a wise man. He sat still and was killed. Gealla was preparing to become a *bean feasa*, a wise woman. She died in response to the threat of being without her soul mate, of catastrophic loss and despair.

In life we must be warriors and wise people and we must learn the difference and when each is appropriate. This is best achieved through the experience of people who have already learned to be wise. It is good for children to spend time in the company of older people, especially their grandparents.

Keith H. Basso (*Wisdom Sits in Places: Landscape and Language*) tells us how the Apache people of Arizona uses landscape features to remind them of their ancient wisdom. The people of Australia walk their story lines, following a string of narrative as they pass various landscape features. We in Sligo have our mountains and carns, our lakes and rivers and their attached stories. It is time to explore these storylines again.

3

FIONNABHAIR, FRAOCH AND THE GREAT WORM

Two carns still stand above Lough Gill, where Oghamra and Romera were put in the body of the earth. In time they became covered in heathers and mosses. The small animals made their homes along with Oghamra, the young man of love and learning, and Romera, the older man of impulse and anger. The cliff and woodland where Gealla and Oghamra had played games and fallen in love grew in reputation as the lake grew in size. Gealla's island had become the academy or field school of Fionnabhair, youngest daughter of Aodh Bán, the local chieftain, a descendant of Aodh Mór.

Fionnabhair by name and bright-headed by nature, this clever young woman had gathered a fine collection of field guides and people of wisdom from centres of experience and learning in Ireland and abroad. They organised and campaigned to form a major college on her island home on the lake for the study and recording of all local flora and fauna and of the way of life of her people. They became scribes for the local chieftains and recorded the story and lore of the district. This project was the major life task and occupation of Fionnabhair. All other matters, of body, mind, spirit and community, fitted into this foundational worldview.

As Fionnabhair grew in grace and favour, her fame for wisdom and genial living spread throughout the country and further afield. Young men and women from all over Europe gathered on her island to share the wealth of knowledge of their people. Horticulture, mariculture, agriculture and bird and animal husbandry and life in the wild were major subjects for study and discussion. Social law and convention, its understanding, interpretation and application to the ever-changing culture of the people, constituted another major area of interest and attention. The visiting students from abroad brought new ideas, beliefs and value systems with them and went back home with fresh thinking and new insights. Fionnabhair's urban and national college brought people together from many places and from many worldviews.

Aodh Bán, a man of great learning and experience, invited many chieftains, bards and druids to visit his Dún, to discuss matters of politics and practice, but also to view Fionnabhair's great centre of learning, in the hope that a suitable husband would present himself to catch the eye of his dusky daughter. Many men came but none found favour to raise a smile or brighten the eye of Fionnabhair. Aodh Bán wondered how far he would have to travel to find a suitable partner for his youngest daughter. Who could please this intense and active woman?

Fraoch, the son of a local hill farmer, was curious to know what brought so many visitors to the island in the lake. He had watched their comings and goings for a long time from the garden of his father's house on the hill above the lake. The safe and secure place of his childhood home was beginning to feel small and enclosed. He began to long for new places and new and stimulating company. It was time to leave. He would travel the world and learn for himself how other people lived and loved before returning to his father's hill farm and heathery hunting grounds. The curious island in the lake could be a good place to begin his expedition, his journey of exploration and adventures. Curiosity had ruled his mind and activities since he was born. He had an ache in the pit of his stomach for the adventure that lay ahead. Where and how far would it take him before it allowed him to return home?

It was late one evening, early in the summer, as the sun was sinking into the sea beyond the mountains to the west, when Fraoch finished his day's work. He walked down the hill with a pack on his back and swam out to the island in the lake to see for himself what was so wonderful about the place. It was an easy, if wet, passage and on the way he convinced himself that it was his right to investigate this mysterious place. He felt drawn to it. He would learn what he could and then move east, crossing the low and purple mountains, turning his back to the setting sun and his life as a boy: tonight, this strange and busy island and tomorrow, the world. He felt a shiver of delight and anticipation flush through his bones.

He arrived on the island shore as Fionnabhair was lighting her wick lamp and soft Beltane shadows brought the cool of evening as a pleasing gift. Fionnabhair combed her hair in the glimmering light of her home fire and hummed softly a new tune she was composing. The tune, for the harp and voice, was intended to celebrate the spring growth of the Great Mother who lived on the mountain in the horizon to the west. She, a daughter of the Mother as much as she was of Aodh Bán, tidied her hair and her mind as she prepared for sleep and to meet the mares of night. She felt happy with her life and grateful to the Great Mother for her gifts of learning among her friends and fellow students, and for this blessed and tranquil place of soft shadows. Life was good and full with promise of a worthwhile life.

Fraoch, kneeling on the shore, let the water run from his clothes while he surveyed the village with a great edifice at its centre. The quiet and lack of activity surprised him. Surely this should be a loud and boisterous place with so many strange people milling about? But it was anything but loud. There were no guard dogs or watching warriors. Did they not expect trouble and strife and commotion? Was he wasting his time coming here to such a dull place where everyone was abed at sundown? Maybe he should look a little further. But what was he looking for? What went on here that was worth his time to investigate?

It seemed, from his vantage point on the shore, that this was a place of peace and learning where no one was expected to come with anything but good intent to visit this island of saints and scholars. He could see torches burning in the village streets and fires flickering through the open windows. He had to find out what was afoot here. A few short strides brought him to the nearest house. It was small and circular, with a pointed roof made of grasses and rushes and a smoke-hole at the centre, supported by a low wall. A sturdy oak door swung on a stout leather hinge on the eastern side of the house and a small window on the western side to view the setting sun and the house of the Great Mother. The door was ajar.

He could hear someone moving about inside. He peeped in to see who was humming so softly. He leaned low and forward to get a better view. He could make out the form of a young woman, sitting and brushing her hair by the fireside. Even in this pale light he could make out soft and smiling features remarkably like those of Aodh Bán, the local chieftain whom he had seen many times at the fairs and summer gatherings at Sligeach. This must be his youngest daughter, the remarkable young woman who had one half of the countryside talking about her and the other half coming to visit her island college.

In his eagerness to see he leaned in more to get a better view. He leaned too far and overbalanced, falling heavily, right at the feet of the beautiful Fionnabhair. She was astonished at this abrupt entry to her house. She grabbed her hair brush to use as a weapon to defend herself and to chase this intruder away.

Fraoch scrambled to his feet and spluttered his apologies to the surprised and disconcerted young woman. She had stopped humming and was now looking fierce, as fierce as a blue-eyed, blonde and rather beautiful young woman could look. Quickly he regained his standing and decorum only to stare open mouthed into the brightest eyes he had ever seen. Grinning sheepishly through his blushes he began to relax and to capitalise on the opportunity that fate had dropped at his feet, or at her feet to be exact. His bungling initiative turned to planning and planning hastily turned to purposeful courtship. So gentle and unpractised was Fraoch at courtship, however, that his tender advances were easily turned aside.

Fionnabhair quickly realised that this gentle young man was no threat to her. She too relaxed as she rather enjoyed watching him trying to regain his composure and the initiative. Fraoch was pressed hard with her quick wit and probing questions about who he was and what he was there for. He stammered half-composed replies and gave ground to the onslaught of Fionnabhair's alacrity. Ardour was no match for Fionnabhair and her rising laughter and wit. He had to back away. He had, in the end, to retreat to the shore of the lake while attempting to regain his sense of balance and decorum. Fionnabhair's counter-play could not be resisted. With one final toss of her hair she toppled Fraoch into the lake. His gentle nature and inexperience had lost the conquest. He was in deep embarrassment.

Fraoch tumbled into and down through the darkening waters, lost to his hillside world of heather, sun and sky and heading into the depths of despair. He could barely see where he was going. His mind was clouded and clear thinking was out of reach. He was out of control. He had no ploy or support to keep him up. Emotions and feelings quickly took over. The need and urge to swim up to the surface was weakened by the thought of again facing Fionnabhair. Her flair and vigour had overwhelmed him. He sank into the pit of nightmare. All sense of time and place slipped away. Despair was near.

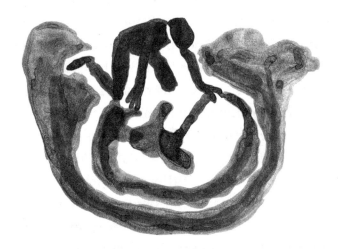

Only one sense remained with him. There was something moving below him, something dark and menacing. He had landed, hit rock bottom, on the back of the Great Worm that lived in that dark and cold pit. The Worm, a relic left behind when the Formorians, the nightmarish demons of earliest times, had retreated to their home under the frozen northern seas after the Maigh Tuireadh battle. Later it had been sustained by the black blood of an angry old warrior who had killed himself in shame a long time ago and by many other acts of dark passion. The Worm had waited for this moment when another, this time a young man overwhelmed with emotions, was driven out of his mind and into to the Worm's lair.

Fraoch could feel the cold hatred of the Worm, a cold-blooded monster that haunted places of ignorance and arrogance out of sight and out of reach of places of learning and love. The two worlds lived side-by-side with only a veil between them, a veil that could be torn by strong emotions and extreme feelings. Passion bridged the breach. Fraoch began to feel another terror also but of a different sort. The laughter of Fionnabhair still rang in his ears. His own longings mingled with a sense of losing all and the Worm was nourished by this dizzying concoction. It ached with the great need of revenge and rage. It longed to consume these over-flowing passions.

Fraoch's clumsy floundering quickly turned to writhing in agony as his frustration grew. Fears and passions rumbled, like thunder, through his body, mind and spirit. He was isolated from all help and support. He had no shelter or weapon to counter the attacking and ravenous Worm. He was not familiar with this type of combat. The Worm drew him to the darkest recesses of the lake bottom and struggled to subdue his soul.

Fraoch weakened slowly as the Darkness and the Worm enfolded him. He felt chilled to the bone. He had lost the battle of wits with Fionnabhair and now he was losing this battle of the spirit with the Worm of Darkness, and he knew it. He felt it. Even his will to fight back was draining away. Darkness and coldness were filling him and he was losing his soul. Rage and long restrained youthful passion flushed through his weakening body. This contradictory mix of power and weakness left him speechless and hopeless. All seemed lost.

Fionnabhair stopped laughing when she realised where Fraoch's despair and distress were drawing him. She could see that he was in deep trouble and it frightened her to think that she, a child of light, could lose this innocent youth to her great enemy, the Worm of Darkness. This was against everything that her island home stood for, all that she strove for. She had to stop this tragedy from coming to realisation. What could she do against such fear and anger, hatred and the lust for revenge?

Instinct informed her. Fionnabhair took a ring from the heart finger of her left hand, a ring once given to her as a reminder of the unending and pure love of her wise and powerful father, the aged and kindly warrior of the soul, Aodh Bán. She threw it to Fraoch as he struggled to find his way out of the clutches of the Worm. Fraoch needed such a weapon to fight this evil creation. The ring flashed as it spun through the air catching the last rays of the setting sun. It held the flash, a sword of light, as it sank into the dark watery depths of the lake. The great point of light illuminated the depths as it spiralled down to where the life and death struggle was in progress. Fraoch saw the ring in the corner of his eye as it tumbled down and lunged to catch it as it came within reach.

With the *claíomh solais*, the sword of light, he lunged at his tormentor and pierced the heart of the Worm. It recoiled in agony and surprise. He watched it as it warped away to the bottom of the watery valley, to where Romera's blackened sword lay at the deepest part of the lake, still stained with his dark blood. It wrapped itself around the sword and licked its wounds. The wound inflicted by the flashing ring was deep and deadly but not fatal. To kill the Worm it would take a sustained war and many such wounds. But that was for another day, for many other days. For now, the Worm stayed very quiet and still, spitting in fury and frustration, and waited for its next opportunity. He would wait and it would surely come.

Fraoch slowly recovered his senses and swam, limp and weak, to the surface of the lake. Ahead he could see the blurred image of the beautiful young and anxious girl kneeling on the edge of the shore. Fionnabhair helped and supported him as he hauled himself ashore and lay on his back on the stones, exhausted, soaked but happy to be back in arms of his new found love. He had lost, at least for the moment, his appetite for journeying and adventure but, as his strength recovered, his appetite for the company of Fionnabhair was growing rapidly. Somehow he knew that his travelling would not be too extensive but his adventures would be many. Fionnabhair's happy eyes were wells deep enough for Fraoch to lose himself in and his love and longing drew him in that direction.

Many stories grew from these wells of inspiration in the eyes of Fionnabhair. The people of Sligo still tell stories of Fionnabhair, the Lady of the Lake, and Fraoch, the young man of the hills, and their children and their children's children still climb to the carns, look across the lake as Fraoch did and fall in love again with Fionnabhair. Her tradition of learning lives on in the people. The little island is now covered with heathers of all hues and many of the other flowers of Fraoch's hill. Innish Fraoch or Inishfree is known worldwide as a place of contemplation and ease, 'where peace comes dropping slow'. It is celebrated in story, song, poetry and film.

The Worm continues to wait.

On Further Reflection

Some of the most powerful natural forces originate inside each one of us. Emotions and feelings can overwhelm us just as a landslide, flood or tsunami can overwhelm our community.

Emotions are the immediate impulses that nature has given us to cope with sudden opportunities and threats. Emotions come from our mind and cultural conditioning.

Feelings are the stored and reinforced emotional responses, a legacy of the opportunities and threat types that have assailed us since conception and, perhaps, to our earlier generations. Feelings are stored in our body, our muscles, organs and bones.

Emotions are associated with younger people who have not, as yet, stored or ingrained enough responses to emotional impulses to have feelings. Besides repetition, traumatic or powerful emotional experiences can generate deeply embedded feelings. The normal responses are fight and flight or sitting still.

Fight is a response deriving from anger. Anger suggests that we have the ability to overcome the threat or to regain a lost opportunity. Anger is the response of the warrior and becomes the normal response if these are experienced often

31

enough. Such stored responses are felt in the body and are called feelings.

Flight is the response deriving from fear where the person is overwhelmed. Getting out of reach of the threat is the impulse for many. It is associated with cowardice in some societies where adult people are seen as defenders of children, older people and resources.

Sitting still is a third option open to those who are mature enough to have developed it. The response of sitting still and not fighting or running away takes a lot of courage and practice. Composure and stolid acceptance comes from long experience of not fighting or running. It may deter any threat or give time to appreciate the true nature of an opportunity.

The Worm is the bad thought, the emotion out of control, the want to do harm to another. Such a worm continues from one generation to another and never dies. The suggestion in the story is that they are the bad thing, the ice core left behind in the bottom of the lake by the retreating ice. The various lake and lough monsters are like the Black Boar on the mountain. They wait for the opportunity to re-emerge.

The *claíomh solais*, the sword of light, is the knowledge and wisdom to do better. It is not always evident but arrives in a flash when needed in times of threat and danger. We must have the courage to grab it and use it when it does come. It usually comes through a friend rather than directly to the one in danger.

The island is the ivory tower where intellectuals live. A select group, separate from the rest of the community, they threaten to form a hierarchical society based on the idea of special knowledge, talents and abilities. It can be a dangerous place to visit unless you know the protocols.

The lake is the collection of emotional forces that must go through the river course, the life experience, to become ready to reach the sea where wisdom collects. The sea is the mix of knowledge and experience, the collective unconscious, that is drawn from by the wise people.

4

MAEBH, WARRIOR CHIEFTAIN

F ar to the west of Lough Gill, beyond the town of Sligo, is
where the Garavogue river, the river of the Garbh O'c, the
Wise Woman, casts its detritus into the sea. There on the edge
of the shore stands Knock na Rea, the noble Hill of the Moon.
This prominent hill dominates the landscape on the western tip
of the Coolera Peninsula, the headland of the Wood of the
Squirrels. The great carn on the hilltop stands as a sentinel,
watching the centuries tick by since the earliest arrivals put it
there to remind them of their dependence on the bounty of the
Great Mother, the Earth. She had nourished many children
long before the tragedy in the time of Aodh Bán, Fraoch and
Fionnabhair.

Their descendants grew in wisdom and strength in the clear view of the Mother. They lived their lives peacefully and easily on her plains, in the forests and beside the streams and rivers. They lived along the shorelines of her rivers and sea and harvested the rich crops that flourished there. They lived in the shadow of the Mother's mountain and hunted her woodlands, built their hearths and raised their children in her glens above her sandy strands.

Maebh was their warrior chieftain. She had married Ailill, a minor chieftain of the cold north, and developed alliances with the other northern chiefs who were then her relatives through marriage. Marriage and alliances were the wise way forward. In this way Maebh confirmed the high status of Connaght as the province of the wisdom absorbed from the red sea of the setting sun. It was brought ashore by the salmon that had soaked it up since birth and released it into the person lucky enough to make a meal of it.

Although Maebh spent a lot of her time at Crúacháin, the seat of the chieftains of Connaght, she loved to linger on the beaches and strands under Knock na Rea and to hunt through the glens and plains of her childhood. In particular, she loved the never-ending hunt on the lowlands of Ben Bulben, the mountain of the Black Boar whose fierce character and blood lust fascinated Maebh. Many of her political and war stratagems were modelled on the plunging attacks of this wild and lusty creature. This was so much the case that Maebh herself took on much of the character of this fierce totem animal of the mountain. Maebh left us a large legacy of stories of her conquests of chieftains and their lands through strategic alliances. Her many conquests generated the popular aphorism:

*'The shadow of the man coming to her fell across the
shadow of the man that was leaving her.'*

She was intoxicated with her love of the lovely province of Connaght which had been gifted to her by the Great Mother. All chieftains of Connaght and all other provinces were initiated into their reign by marrying the Mother. This was how they were empowered, as in marrying the Mother they became responsible for all her children, all who lived locally in her creation. Marriage legitimated their rule and gave them the authority to act on behalf of the best interests of the family of her people.

Maebh became an icon of the Mother because of her many attributes gifted to her from the Mother. She became chieftain and advocate for the Mother when she was selected and acclaimed by her people. Chieftains were selected by the 'wise people of the clan', all those in the later stage of their life. If the chieftain, man or woman, remained whole, not injured in battle or hunting, they could be nominated again seven years later. They presented themselves to their people from an elevated site, offering their services. The 'wise people', those past the years of child-bearing for women and the years of hunting for men, cried out to accept their offer. They were acclaimed. Their offer was rejected by the 'wise people' if they turned their backs to them and remained quiet. This is at the root of the story of the Lia Fáil, the Stone of Destiny at Tara, where provincial chieftains were elevated if considered suitable to being responsible for the whole island of Ireland.

Maebh's most famous story concerned her attempt to buy the great bull of Cooley from a chieftain of the northeast. She wanted the bull so that she could hold equal rank with her husband in the area of husbandry. She was already equal to

36

Ailill in stocks of cows, sheep and pigs, but his battling white bull, the Finnbhenach, was outstanding, better than any in her herd. She knew of the Cooley Bull as northern Cooley already had a long tradition and high reputation for raising belligerent bulls.

Maebh sent emissaries to buy the bull, the one with an outstanding reputation for combativeness and fierceness. A price was negotiated, hands were shaken and a deal that was fair to all was done. Everyone was happy. Everybody relaxed and paid attention to the Brehon laws of hospitality. Sleeping places were allocated, food and drinks were shared, stories were told, songs were sung and music and dance enjoyed. A little more *uisce beatha,* whiskey, was called for and consumed. That was a mistake. 'A closed mouth never broke a nose' and 'a still tongue never broke a tooth' are old sayings among our people, and would have been good advice for a member of Maebh's cohort, but he was inclined to have a big mouth and a sharp tongue.

'It was lucky that we could peacefully conclude this deal,' said one of Maebh's emissaries.

'Peacefully! Lucky! What can you mean?' The Cooley contingent was astonished and angered but worse was to follow.

'Well. If you would not have sold the bull to us we would have been compelled to take it, deal or no deal.'

'Take it! Compelled! What an insult. You cannot have the bull now under any circumstances. Cooley cannot be seen to accede to such demeaning insults.'

Everything changed in an instant. The agreement was revoked. The neutral camp was, in moments, in turmoil. The way of wisdom – proposal, discussion and agreement – was lost. Friendship and hospitality changed to hostility and the need to get away. War, the usual mode of operations of the northern contingent, was re-established. The numbers of northern warriors in the camp greatly outnumbered the western contingent. Maebh's warriors backed up to the wall, side-stepped to the door and moved in haste to get away from the camp as quickly as possible.

Noses and much more were in danger. Distance was needed to prevent deeper insults and bloodshed. Negotiations were no longer possible and any attempt to negotiate would cause delay, raise tempers and possibly lead to bloodshed. What could be done now? The western warriors could not go back to Maebh empty-handed. Something had to be done. Some new approach was needed, but what and when?

With the negotiations out of reach only one other process could be adopted. The body of the western warriors now planned to capture the mighty brown bull by force. Maebh needed this bull, the symbol of battle prowess, to show that she could stand as an equal with the other provincial chieftains. Wisdom alone was not enough if she was to become the central power in the landscape.

If normal commerce, along with music, song and dance, could not gain what was required, perhaps some show of power would. All four tactics were needed if Maebh was to be the chief of chieftains at Tara. Her warriors needed to demonstrate their worth and display their mettle. But Maebh's warriors met their match and more when they faced the northern Red Branch and their champion, Cú Chulain, the mighty Hound of Ulster, at the site of the Yellow Ford in the territory of Midhe, Meath. Pride was sacrificed on the altar of arrogance and vanity and another lesson had to be learned.

'Do not threaten violence on people who live by violence.'

The battle raged and alternated between single and mass combat. Many good warriors died that awful day. Although Maebh eventually gained possession of the brown bull, the Dun Cúiligne, the cost had been very high, too high. Was the prize worth the terrible price? Many thought not. The northerners and the westerners counted and carried away their valiant dead on their shields. But who had won?

The Cú of Chulain was dead. Badhbh, the war crow, had picked out his eye when she landed on his shoulder to check if any life and menace remained in him. He was dead and yet he would live forever in story. The surly Red Branch withdrew from the battle field and headed north to Émáin Macha, Armagh, to tend their wounded.

Maebh's warriors straggled back to Rath Crúacháin with some of her best on their shields, ready for the funeral fires. A brooding Maebh was left with ample time to salve her wounds and count her losses. She was angry with her ambassadors who had handled negotiations so carelessly at the end, but she was wise enough not to let them go raiding ever again. She spent the rest of her life in Connaght, around Crúacháin, Ben Bulben and the Hill of the Moon, hunting deer and wild boar and coaching her many grandchildren.

In time the wounds of war healed but some other things did not. The brown bull did not settle well at Crúacháin. True to its nature it fought with Finnbhenach, Ailill's white bull, and eventually escaped heading again to its home on the Cooley Peninsula. War never sits easily with wisdom.

Although Maebh was never defeated in any battle she was often stretched and drawn. For Maebh conquest was not a possibility. For her nobody could take or own land. Land belonged to the clan and her task was to take good care of it for them.

Her intoxication with the land of her birth was manifest in all her actions. Her feisty nature kept Ailill busy pouring oil on troubled waters. Her vigour spent itself in adventure and the incessant hunt. Her name, Maebh, derives from the ancient word for this passion and love of the land. It was to show itself many times in the history of the world.

It is surprising that Maebh, a woman of action, died an old woman in her own bed. Upon her death her body was tied to a pillar stone on the top of her favourite hill above the estuary at Knock na Rae. Even in death she stood with the Mother, in full battle dress, facing her real enemies in the north. She lives on in the minds of the people, overlooking the estuary, where the river gifts its life experiences to the sea.

On Further Reflection

Maebh was the symbol of the Earth axis, at the Fir Bolg druid tree centre at Uisneach's Aill na Muireann, the Rock of Divisions, and exhibited all the attributes of the chieftain in perfect balance. Such is the nature of the true chieftain as described in the Brehon Laws. The basis of the law was that the chieftains were the selected leaders by the elders of their people. They could not take office until they had been acclaimed by their people and then only for a period of seven years. During that period of stewardship, the chieftain was held responsible for the welfare of the people and all the wealth in the environment.

If it was a good harvest everybody sang the chieftain's praises and if the harvest was bad everyone complained about their ill favour with the Great Mother. She remained central, reflecting an earlier time when the protection of mothers and their children was the all-important duty of the local community. Times were changing when Maebh was chieftain. The male members of the community were changing from outranging hunters and were becoming warriors that guarded the borders of their hunting and gathering lands. Ideas of ownership and kingship were arising and the Brehon Laws were changing to reflect this.

Maebh reflected, to some degree, the earlier Fir Bolg value and belief system. She represented the Great Mother with her warrior face, the face that shed her blood in bringing her children into the world. In time she would become more like Fionnabhair or Gealla, dependant on the good will of the male warrior group. In the meantime a transitional face was necessary.

Maebh, this intoxicating woman, followed in the footsteps of one even more ancient and exciting – Brí, the Mór Riaghain, the Great Mother who lived for millennia before Maebh but the two of them have become synonymous in the minds of our people. The names changed as new people arrived with their own stories, but the foundational story remained.

Maebh married each of the High Chiefs of the other four provinces. As the symbol of the centre, of responsibility, and above all, of wisdom in the community, she drew on the characteristics of all the provincial chieftains. Uisneach was her rightful home where she stood beside the great stone at the centre of the original five provinces and was an icon that symbolised the Earth Mother for her people. As such she also symbolised the characteristics inherent in the four provinces surrounding Tara, in the central province of authority and responsibility in Midhe.

Ulster, in the north, was the symbol of battle and military prowess – still a touch of it there? Munster, in the south, was the symbol of music, song and dance. Long live the Kerry dancers. Leinster, in the east, was the symbol of trade and commerce. Our main seaports are still on the east coast. Connaght, in the west, was the symbol of wisdom. Where else, I ask? The Shannon, the major river, and many others bring this wisdom to the sea on the western coast. This wisdom soaks into the salmon that bring it back to shore for the consumption of later generations.

In first marrying Ailill, a minor chief of the North, Maebh, as the Great Mother, was seen to make a truce with the Dark Lords of Winter. As a result, each year, when winter came, they would allow many of Maebh's children to survive their onslaught. They would not kill all but only the weakest. It was this ability to be wise and make compromise that marked Maebh's reign and made her fame live forever.

5

THE FOUR DOORS OF SLIGO

Mountains restrict all travel through the Shelly Place at Sligo. However, easy access is possible through mountain doors at the four major points of the compass. Each door has a colour associated with it as the sun shines from that direction: Grey is the colour of the eastern sky at dawn; white is the colour of the summer sky in the south; red is the colour of the sky as the sun sets in the west and black or blue-black, the colour of the northern night sky.

Bare Ben Bulben's brow towers over the north of Sligo. The black boar is clearly seen in the shape of the mountain as it is approached from Sligo in the south. The long snout still juts out to the sea at Drumcliff, Druim na Cliabh, the Ridge of Rush Bundles. In ancient times the Dark Lords lived behind this mountain, the lords of nature that fought the Mother and helped to shape the world. All was in darkness and frozen at the back of this mountain. Winter, war and withering lived and died there permanently.

At the western end of the mountain, where the boar's snout runs to the sea, there is a narrow passage way between the mountain and the sea. It is called the Black Door through which, in early times, all that was evil and harmful to the children of the Mother was known to arrive. This was the road taken by the Dark Lords, the Fomorians, when they came to devastate the Mother's children. They occupied the warmer and gentler lands of Sligo and devastated the land further south until Lugh, the Sun God, and his warriors of Light of the Tuatha de Danaan, drove Balor and his cold-hearted Formorian marauders back to the north after the first great battle of Maigh Tuireadh. The north was known as the place of darkness that swallowed the sun every night and every winter. It was the black place of death where cold-hearted Balor, the Dark Lord, ruled in the hell of bitterness and hardship.

The Black Door leads from Tory, the island home of Balor of the Evil Eye, the Dark Lord of the North. Tory was the island outpost of the Formorians. This unfathomable place was acknowledged as the abode of all that was evil. It was the antithesis of land and light, sun and sky where Bilé was chieftain. The land was taken back by Lugh and given to Brigit, his sister, the Sun Goddess who cleared it of all that was cold, hard and evil. From this dark place morning sun comes each day and after each winter solstice, pale and weak from its sojourn in the Dark Place.

Fionn, a successor of Lugh, comes around the other end of the mountain of the Black Boar, Ben Bulben, originally Ben Gulbáin. The name Gulbáin translates as 'the big snout'. Each morning Fionn leads his hounds, Bran and Sceolán, on the unending hunt, repeating and reinforcing the outcome of the first Maigh Tuireadh battle. Fionn, his hunting dogs and whole entourage raise a great bird shout marking the victory of the sun and the defeat of the dark night. All creatures join this dawn chorus in celebration of life and light.

The hunting dogs, creatures of light and shade, lead the way. Bran, a white and tawny creature, runs side-by-side with Sceolán, a black and white creature, who always live 'ar scáth a céile', in each other's shadow. So silent are these twins of the trail that they can run at full speed through the forest without making a sound or disturbing a twig, a leaf or a blade of grass. Fionn follows in his chariot of the sky drawn by the mares of morning with a full retinue in hot pursuit. And it was here, under Lug na Gall, that Fionn found Oisin, his son by Saba, the White Lady of Moonlight, daughter of Danube, the River Goddess of Europe and Cernunus, the Stag Lord of the Great Forest.

Oisin, whose name means Little Fawn, was brought here by his mother from the Hill of Allen in Kildare when she was taken hostage by the Dark Lord of the Black North. He had captured her by guile and threat and stole her away from the home she had shared with Fionn at the white-walled fort of Almu in Kildare. It was on this same mountain where Fionn spent most of his later life when his strength and spirit began to decline. Some say that he spent his final days looking for Saba, the love of his young life, and some say that he was still battling to the end with the Dark Lord who had stolen her away.

The Hazel Wood of Sligo covers the edge of the plains below the limestone mountain and is the home of the Great White Sow who suckles her young in the early morning sun. This mother of the Black Boar is at her fiercest when she protects her young, and yet, it is the same mother who will cull her farrows in the years when scavenging is scarce and harsh winds chill the bone on the hills. In good years hazelnuts and acorns made good nourishment for her growing litter. They could grow in wisdom and strength but not always in grace, as the Black Boar signifies. Mother Earth had a nature that could be gracious and kind, like Saba, or dark and savage like the White Sow. Her children always live in jeopardy.

Above this mountain the hinge of the world swings clockwise and forms the pivot point for the wheel of the night sky. The constellations of stars and the wandering planets revolve about this fixed point and provide a clock to measure and mark time. Each day the sun traverses the sky in a chariot drawn by horses and at night the moon and stars reflect the way of life of the people. Many of the names of the night sky characters are now lost but some remain. An Grian, the daytime and mature Sun God, is the original warrior to raze the night and winter. An Geallach, the Bright One, younger sister to An Grian, lights the nights sky and guides the stars to their resting place in the west. An Budduch , keeper of the Pleiades, the herd of young cows and Taurus the bull, would take his wards to summer pasture on the plains of the Shelly Place and to Coill na hIorra, the wood of squirrels, on the other side of the lake.

Sliabh Dá Éan, the Mountain of Two Birds, lies to the east of Sligo. On top of Sliabh Dá Éan there is a small but bottomless lake. If you swim down you eventually surface in the nearby Lough Gill.

To this day the old people say that nothing good comes from the east, reflecting the Viking hoards that came on the east wind to raid and pillage the country. The Grey Door stands in the eastern landscape and through this door arrives the first grey light of dawn. The hills here are in shadow until the sun rises and it is by this door that all things new and un-known have arrived to disrupt the peace and tranquillity of Sligeach, the Shelly Place. But it is also the place where Spring comes from. However, all new things are always difficult and most people wish that things would stay as they are in Spring even when they bring hope for a good Summer.

It was over this eastern mountain that the aged Fionn came on his hunt for the two innocents, Diarmait of the dimpled face and Gráinne of the sunny disposition, when they took shelter in the hills above Glencar. His meanness of spirit lost him much respect when his bad thoughts allowed him to let the healing waters leak through his fingers, and so allowed Diarmait to die of the deep wounds inflicted by the Black Boar of the mountain.

The Grey Door shows most clearly when the new moon rises behind the mountain. On its slopes grow great forests of blackthorn, the tree of magic and blasting. Even these trees lose their blossoms when the east wind blows.

Fionn still swings through this Grey Door at dawn, through the hoop of Fáinne Geal an Lae, the bright ring of morning that forms the entry of the new day. Bran, the tawny hound of the mountain, and Sceolan, grey and mottled hound of the deep glens, race ahead of Fionn's chariot, hunting out their darting quarry in the pale light of dawn. Fionn's great chariot comes charging through Glen Aodh and Glen Cár with Fionn standing on the centre beam, glorious in his shining robes. Following the Fianna, all screaming and shouting in the joy of the chase, comes every creature who rides with them heralding the birth of the new day. This happens every morning still but few people are there to see it now that the world is so intent on its own race to the future. But young Fionn lives on, in the high plains above Glencar.

Knock na Rae, the Hill of the Moon, the noble hill of rays from the setting sun and moon, is keeper of the soft Autumn winds. Maebh, the Mother of all that is, still stands under her great carn on the top of this mountain, facing her enemies in the north. She is the greatest western warrior, the collector of tokens and men's bones, the spiller of blood, her own in childbirth and of all those around her. She even caused best friends Cúchullain and Ferdia to fight to the death in her honour. She is a woman of raging passions that, like Fionn, spent her later life hunting in the moonlight in the hills of Sligo. Upon her mountain where the reddest of suns set and floods the sea blood-red as, like Fionn, it gives its life's blood in death. Fionn was so ashamed and dishonoured by the death of Diarmait that he sailed into the setting sun, opened his veins to the sea, gave his flesh to the fish and his bones to the shore. Many years later his bones were washed in at Cumeen strand. The local people collected them and made a carn at An Cearthu Mór, Carrowmore, the big portion of land used for hostings and gatherings, both social and spiritual ritual.

Knock na Hur, Cnock na hIorra, the Hill of the Squirrels, beyond Moheraboy, Maighera Bui, the Yellow Plain, is known as the site of the second battle of Maigh Tuireadh, between the Fir Bolg and the Danáan Lords of Light. Eochaid Óll-Athair, a chieftain of the Fir Bolg has his carn at the seashore near Balisodare, Beal Easa Daire, the Mouth of the Cataract at the Oak Wood. Although he lost the battle he was commemorated to help appease his troops so as to make a final peace.

The Giant's Grave at the foot of the hill, at the edge of Maighera Bui, is said by story-tellers to be where the bones of Fionn Mac Cumhal are piled. In an earlier time he had shape-shifted to become Lugh, Grandson of Balor, who fought the Dark Lords of the North. Who knows who walked and hunted this land in ancient times? They left their footprints in the sands at Culleenamore and sang their songs of praise in the evening light near Lios Toghal, the place of selections, on top of Fionn's bones at Carrowmore. If you listen carefully you can hear them, and their hounds and hunting horns, as they ride through Glencar or sing songs around their campfire in the Fairy Glen. They still follow the Great Stag and the Black Boar in the stories of the ongoing battle of the Elementals.

On Sliabh Dhamh, the Mountain of the Ox, the White Door stands as sentinel on the southern Sligo border at the entrance to Ladies Brae. Soft summer breezes coming from the south warm the land and bring the crops and fruits to fullness. Hazel trees grow by the tumbling mountain streams and drop their nuts into pools of wisdom and reflection. Here in south Sligo stands Knock na Shí, the Fairy Mountain that guards the pass where elves and pookas play all day along the stony paths. Sunbeams dance in and out through the fairy throng while tall daffodils overflow with honey and cream that is collected from them and the yellow buttercups and cow-slips. Brí lives here as chieftain of the fairies.

Everyone sings here, the *gealtrai* of spring brightness, the *suantrai* of summer joy and the *góltrai* of autumn melancholy. Nobody grows old here but some do wander off and become lost in the world of the big people. The lucky few find their way back to dance the night away and to yawn and stretch in the new light of the bright ring of morning.

The Red Door of the west is the place of the setting sun, made red by the blood of the dying Fionn. Out there, beyond the ninth wave, is the place of death and rebirth, of magic and mystery. Who know what may lie to the west. Maybe even another world.

The four colours of the four directions are still used by many people. Red, white and blue are the colours of many flags. These banner colours represent countries such as the USA, Britain and France. Very few people know the origin of these colours. It was the early or pre-Celtic people of Europe who first recognised these colours. It was part of the colour schemes used to demark social order and levels of responsibility of the all their people. In early Christian tradition, grey, the colour of untreated sheep's wool, was worn by young entrants to the priesthood. Black is still the colour of priests' robes while red and black are in the dress of cardinals, the senior men in the church. White is the colour of the pope's robes even today. The old stories give us a lot of narrative about what changes and what does not.

So many stories; so many colours; so many shades of truth to tell!

On Further Reflection

This story explains itself. We have only to remember and celebrate it, to honour our ancestors. We do this best by telling their stories.

6

BEEZIE'S ISLAND

Age brings its own grace and gravitas. A full life, well lived, brings contentment and wisdom. Great age is the time of teaching, storytelling and silence, philosophy and listening, reflection and the care of small children. Contentment comes from accepting the world as it is. Wisdom comes from the life experience of trying to change the things we can, accepting the things we cannot and knowing the difference. Old age is the quiet phase beyond the years of action. It keeps the body still and close to the hearth. Telling and re-telling stories, old stories that hold the wisdom of the ages, to growing, eager and questioning children allows intuitive knowledge and insight to develop and enables wisdom and contentment to grow by living life on a daily basis.

Life begins in the womb, flows through the birth canal and moves on into the river of life and the still pool of eventual death. In the same way the watercourse begins in the lake, flows through the river and gathers in the sea. In Sligo, the Shelly Place, the watercourse begins in Lough Gill, flows through the Garavogue River and on to the sea in Sligo bay. Gealla, the young Lady of the Lake, lives on her pleasant islands and flows through the Narrows, a turbulent run of water between one of the smaller islands and the shore, running on to become the Groaning Old Crone who staggers past the Hazel wood, under the nippled hill of Carns.

In Abbey-quarter, close to the estuary, the water moves faster making ready for the jump the salmon weir at the Back River. Here it tumbles and troubles itself over the wide and rocky shallows before coming to rest and ease in the deep, dark swirling pools of the estuary at Cartron. The bay spreads between the headlands of *Leath-ros*, Strandhill, and *Béal Easa Dara*, Ballisodare, along the long legs of the Great Mother who stands on the hilltop of Knock na Rae.

The watercourse represents the tract from the womb to the tomb and the adventure from youth and beauty to age and wisdom. It is the experience of this tract that brings with it the detritus of wisdom that gathers in the sea. This store of wisdom has been guarded for future generations by the Warrior Woman who stands sentinel on the Mountain of the Moon, high above the estuary. Salmon live in the sea, soak up knowledge and wisdom, and travel up river bringing their accumulated wisdom with them to re-distribute to the people who live along the shorelines and in the town.

Gealla, with her bright face of youth and beauty and the first face of the Great Mother and spring, lived on the islands of the lake. Her story is as fresh today as it was when she set up her academy, library and college. The inspiring face of the moon rises above the lake and sheds its yellow light, always straight into the eye of the beholder. The new moon rising looks forward and brings good fortune and health to the locality and is the right time to plant and cultivate the land and gardens. The turned head of the full moon gives full face to the river and lights the way to the sea. The old moon looks back over her shoulder remembering its life-journey to the sea.

When the frost is on the grass and the old moon sits in the new moon's lap, the future is contemplated as the voyage ahead. The moon on its back indicates that hard times are ahead with snow and frost to come. Such weather signs can also apply to life. Old people pay great attention to them and prepare for what is forecast.

The adventure and battle of life, in bringing children into the world, teaching and training them in the ways of their people, is embodied in the carn where the Great Mother resides. Today she is called Maebh but in earlier times she was known as Brí, the source of life and fertility. Brí or buí, is the colour of the flowers in spring and also the brightness of the moon at night, and the face of the daughter of the Great Mother. Daghda, her father, stands with Lugh, her life partner, on the hill on the other side of Sligo town, on Carns Hill that overlooks the lake. He is the Great Father figure noted for his fecundity and his large club or nightstick that furrows the ground as he drags it behind him. He, like Brí or Maebh, has had many life partners. They make formidable figures in the landscape.

Oghma, son of the Daghda, is also commemorated on Carns Hill. This young man reflects Oghamra and Fraoch, but his story is older. He was the divinity of the early form of writing; the original Ogham lettering developed to denote harp music but which later became a way of writing script, usually on marker stones. The old wisdom was considered too valuable to risk writing it down. Written script can be read quietly and spoken out loud, but this does not mean that the narrative is understood by the reader or speaker. Also, if written down, it can be changed by those who do not have the true wisdom that it contains. For this reason, wisdom was learned in long dog-gerel verse with a structure and assonance that made it difficult to cover up any alteration made to it.

Old age and experience follows the course of the river, the Garavogue, named after the Garb O'c, the Woman of Wise Years. The river, representing life experience, is the third face of the Mother. She, as Grandmother and Autumn, raised the young children while their birth-mother hunted and gathered alongside their birth-father. Later years also brought the re-sponsibility, for men past hunting years and women past child-bearing years, of selecting and affirming leaders of the clan or people of the valley, *an clúin,* where they lived.

When I was a young child, living in this mysterious landscape, an old lady of the lake would arrive on the banks of the river, near where I lived, each Saturday at high noon. For me she was a magical being. Her clothes and broad-brimmed hat were of an earlier generation and her demeanour was such that she seldom spoke. She had a sharp and pointed look about her. She was a formidable woman, tough and strong, independent and wise, able and mobile. She would arrive from her island home on the lake in her small, clinker-built boat and step ashore at the landing stage near the weir.

My family and friends lived here, close to where we fished for little speckled trout and shining perch when the broad-winged mayfly was on the river. We were scared of otters biting our ankles in the gloaming of a May evening. The older boys told us to put cinders in our rubber boots so that the otter would let go sooner when the crunch of cinders fooled it into thinking a bone had been crunched. This was their way of trying to keep the river fish to themselves.

Here, where the river slows and pours its wealth of bubbles and bracken over the weir into its final stretch on its run to the sea, the old woman of the lake would tie up her boat with its slim outboard engine. Me and my fellow warriors would come to spell-bound attention and gaze in wonder at this woman of legend and mystery that ruled the lake from the Narrows to the mouth of the Bonnet at Druim Dhá hÉthir, the Ridge of the Two Demons at Dromahair. We waited and watched and stood guard on her craft while she would disembark, tighten her scarf around her neck, collect her many carrier bags and make her way to town to buy her week's supply of groceries. She never spoke to any one of us. At best she just looked at us in a way that stuck us to the ground. We did not dare leave. We simply took responsibility for her clinker-built river-boat and fittings until she returned loaded down with supplies. These were ferried back to where her boat lay in wait, bobbing in the shallows in the shadow of the wall at the riverside.

She was Beezie, little Brigit Gallagher, an ancient woman made of iron, who lived on one of the larger islands on Lough Gill that today still holds her name. She was old even when my big brother stood guard for her. She was old even when God was a boy and the world was new. For me, she was Gealla, Fionnabhair, Maebh and the Garbh O'c all rolled into one. She was mysterious and awesome. She spoke to few and minded her own business.

She had the company of the fishermen and game hunters who frequented the lake in winter. The shooting season, start-ing in November each year, was the beginning of her social season. Duck and rabbit satisfied the younger hunters while woodcock and pheasant filled the bag of men on a good day. The salmon season, beginning on New Year's Day each year, brought more men to her lake through the Narrows as they set out to find the magical fish. Salmon were a species apart. Other fish, ordinary fish – trout, perch, eel and bream – were for cooking and eating whereas catching salmon was a social event; selling it was a commercial event; eating it was totally mystical and talking about the catch was a ritual that bestowed great status on the lucky fisherman. Women did not fish or hunt and any who did were looked on with suspicion and seen as, somehow, strange or foreign.

The only woman legitimately involved in hunting and fishing was Beezie. She was keeper of the lake and islands. Meeting Beezie was part of a rite of passage to manhood and bestowed a right to take a boat on the lake. An introduction to her was achieved simply by catching her eye when she came to town, being seen by her and eventually having your existence acknowledged by her. If she knew your name and family and actually spoke to you, you were of the inner circle.

Delivering a small gift to her door on the island was restricted to a small number of older fishermen. I never reached such august heights of social prestige. The world changed before I could aspire to that. Mine was limited to that of a small wide-eyed boy who guarded her boat and felt privileged to do so. The gift, usually a bottle of whisky or beer, recognised the fact that the lake belonged to Beezie and we went there only at her invitation. Although legally this was not true, socially and culturally it was imperative.

Beezie's house and garden were out of bounds, taboo places like the carns on the hilltops, reserved for powerful adults. It was dangerous and foolish to go there. It was fatal to damage any part of such magical landscapes. You always brought something with you when you did go near to them. 'Never arrive with one arm as long as the other' was the basic rule when you went to visit anyone or any place.

When going to visit Maebh you brought a small stone to add to her carn. As a child, when visiting Beezie's island you brought nothing material. You brought company and laughter and games to play in front of her house. She would look out to see what was going on but would never interfere. If children were doing childish things they were allowed to display their innocence. Any inappropriate activity was too scary to contemplate. Who knew what might happen if you upset Beezie's sense of propriety. In summer children picnicked on her island and would pay their respects but always at a distance. Visits to Beezie's house were not appropriate. In any case, it was too scary. We played our childish games of imagination and innocence and kept her amused during the long summer school holidays.

This iconic woman was surrounded by men of high status. She served to set foundational thoughts about women. Like Maebh on the Knock na Rae, Beezie gave us ideas of the mystery of womanhood and female power. Far from being the weaker sex, women were in charge of all things social and political. Men, like children who merely minded her boat, provided whatever tool the woman might need or use. This social order or community reflected the matri-centred world of Brí or Maebh.

Men continued to hunt for fish, birds or small game and brought them home to the table, as they did in ancient times. You never took anything away from the carn or the island. Everything was sacrosanct. Everything was intact, whole and holistic in the original sense of the word. Everything held part of the soul of the place in the modern sense of the word.

Beezie died tragically many years later in a fire at her house. The fishermen brought back the news that stunned the whole community and laid a pall over Sligo that has never fully cleared. An era came to an end when Beezie passed into the Otherworld. The lake had always been a thin place where this world and the Otherworld were only lightly veiled from each other. For the people of my generation it was even thinner. Beezie still lives on her island in the minds of people like me and in the local history and folklore of the lake. We wait for her to go shopping again.

'Ni bheidh a leithéad arís ann!
[We will never see the likes of them again!]

Even now I can feel the sense of pride we felt when we guarded her boat. She helped us to learn how to be responsible and respectful of people of age and experience. To this day, I would not dare to ignore any older person in need of care or assistance. This would be a disgrace that would be a blemish on the reputation of any family. Even if no one else knew of or witnessed the misdemeanour, Beezie might still be watching.

And so the story of the women of Sligo continues.

On Further Reflection

This story is real. It explains itself. We have only to remember and celebrate it.

7

A SONG OF TUAN

A dhaoine uaisle, a cáirde gaelach,
Is mise bhur seanchai!

[My fine people, friends of Ireland,
I am your storyteller!]

I am your storyteller. Think of me as someone so old that it is difficult to say if I am man or woman or some being created just to tell this story.

People gather at the crossroads of the world to dance, sing and to hear my stories. My stories are more precious than gold and older than story telling. *Is ceart an rud é. [It is a true thing.]*

I am Tuan.
I am legend.
I am memory turned to myth.

It is appropriate that my story today is told to people from around the world. My story is universal. My story is ancient. My story is eternal. Like all good stories my story will make you laugh with joy, cry with sadness and sigh with ease.

My people came from the east out of the plains of Africa, the mountains of Asia and the forests of Europe. We learned the wisdom that comes only from experience and followed the sun and the rivers looking for where our people could have peace, abundance and contentment. Our earliest journey to the north, out of Africa, is lost in the mists of my mind and lives only in the spirit of my people. *Is sean an scéal é. [This is an old story.]*

We came west, from the great subcontinent of towering mountains, tormented rivers and vast plains until we reached Asia Minor and the valley between the two great rivers. This was our resting place, the place where we transformed ourselves to become Europeans. We made our home there for many generations. We discovered Spirit and learned to live together. We developed language, laws, poetry, music, song and dance. We enjoyed sport and the competition of friends. We lived well.

Ár brithar beo, our spoken language, one of the oldest spoken tongues in Europe, developed our culture and social order and spread throughout the Old World. Although confined to the western edge of Europe today, it still shares many words with Sanskrit which is now a language only of scholars and mystics of the east. *Is iontach an scéal é. [It is a wondrous story.]*

Ansin, we moved further west again, to the great lake, the Black Sea. We lived there for many turns of the sun and moon but still we longed for the land of heart's desire. We continued to search feeling the need for it. Our people divided here. Some went north, on the sunrise side of the lake, following the sun again to find its resting place. They went so far north that they lost the sun and settled along the northern seacoast. They populated the northern half of Europe, all the way to Scandinavia. These northern nomads, toughened from living on the edge of the ice sheets lightened in colour and complexion and grew tall and straight. They quietened from living hand to mouth in the frozen wastes. Moving west and then south they came through the northern islands on their way to this, their new island home.

The main group, the Tuatha Dé Danaan, followed the Great River named for Danu, the water spirit, and then along the minor river, the Rhine. They left many children behind each time they moved. Those resolved to go all the way continued sailing west through the heart of Europe to the coast before crossing to Britain and then to the Isle of the Blest. They sailed up the Boyne River and settled in the fertile midland plains.

Another group, the Sons of Mil, travelled south of the Black Sea, sailing along the sunlit coasts of the inland sea, the Mediterranean, to reach the eastern coast of Iberia. They sailed up the Ebro River, shouldered their boats across the mountains of the Pyrenees and camped on the edge of the western sea at La Coruña. Many of my people stayed behind on the northern coast of Iberia and watched their children prosper and grow strong. But some were still restless and wanted to go on to the edge of the world. Those who stayed behind cried salt tears as they watched their sons and daughters, with great red billowing sails, lift on the rising tide and sail into the mouth of Oengus, the Sun God of my people.

Oengus laughed and danced with joy at the courage of his children as they sought the Promised Land over the edge of the world. He led the way out through the Pillars of Hercules into the great ocean on the salmon sea road that leads only to the abyss. Oengus and the ocean were kind to them and brought them safely to the western shores of the Isle of the Blest, a home fit for heroes. He must have laughed again later when he saw their children's children launch themselves into the great void of space to reach his sister, Brigit, *an Ghealach*, the Bright One, the Lady of the Night. *Is deas an smaoineamh é. [It is a nice thought.]*

As Oengus, I had witnessed the forming of the earth and was its guardian. The great Bilé, Lord of the Universe, sent me to watch over and care for his wife and my mother, the beautiful Brigit, Mother of all creation, the Doni, the Danu, spirit of the lakes, rivers, the sea and of life. *Is álainn an radharc é. [It is a beautiful view.]*

As a great salmon I led my people along the sea corridor, the salmon road that brought them to the edge of the world. Finally, I brought them to the west coast of my beloved land, the Isle of the Blest, over-flowing with milk and honey, the Promised Land, fit for a noble people who had made the great journey. This land was where the Bright One slept each day while I watched over my people. I saw their ships come out of the mist of the sea or the sky: I cannot be sure which now that memory fades and I have become merely human. *Is ceart an caoi é. [It is the right way for sure.]*

I shape-changed again and floated in the sky on the wings of a great sea eagle and watched as they burned their ships. This was their symbol that their journey of discovery was over and now they could rest on the breast of Brigit and grow to be the makers of history and the shapers of worlds. I had peeled the skin of ice from my island and watched Brigit plant and nourish this emerald in the western sea joined to the sky by mist and mystery.

My people came in great waves. Their earliest book, the *Book of Takings*, tells of the Fomorians, the Nemedians, the Parthalonians, the Milesians, the Fir Bolgs and the De Danaans who all came to this land of promise and plenty. Each in their own way met Brigit and her sisters and worked hard to earn the right to stay and live in peace in this land of beauty. *Nach deas an sceal é? [Is this not a good story?]*

I shape-changed again and roamed the purple hills as a Great Stag and watched them as they cleared the forest and make lakes and plains to make room for their children and their children's children. They ringed the trees to make nemetons to ease the hunt and eventually to corral the bigger animals. Farming came later, crops of grass and grain and roots. They lived well in a woman-centred world. In general my children were good and generous of spirit, jealous of rivals, honourable in their dealings and always ready to sing and dance and celebrate the joy of living. In teenage years they were troublesome and they often settled their differences in battle, either real or mock. They had seven battle levels.

First was to explain to the opponent that the difference of opinion was leading to a problem. The *second* level was to send a small group to discuss the political or philosophical difference and to try to find a compromise. The *third* level was to send a selected hero to do combat for them, mock and then real. The hero would display his battle skills before the door of the opponent. The opposing community could accede at this stage. The *fourth* level was to have the implied challenge taken up by a member of the opposing community. The winner claimed victory in the argument as well as the fight. If the challenge was not taken up the *fifth* level was fulfilled by a selection of heroes joining the displaying hero and threatening to over-run the opposing community. If the opposing community did not concede a selection of opposing heroes could take up the challenge and engage in bloody battle. If they didn't the *sixth* level was to have the full communities face each other until one surrendered or else the *seventh* level, all-out warfare, ensued. Most battles seldom went past level three. Concession at any stage settled the difference. The battles were a way of solving differences, either legal or philosophical. A hero could be a philosopher or a warrior. Graciousness in everything helped to alleviate the injury to pride or to physical bodies.

But, as in all families, some of my children became mean of spirit. They would not share fairly all that I had given them. The children of the north had grown cold in their hearts from time spent near the ice fields. They had become frightened and insecure wanting all that they saw for their own. They lost respect for Brigit, for each other and treated my gifts with familiarity, scorn and disrespect, and held their brothers and sisters in bondage. In the 1800s this led to the diaspora of our people. They left in large numbers to avoid death and disease and went to the ends of the earth to find my peace. *Sé fáth mo bhuartha. [It is the cause of my deep sadness.]*

More than eight million children lived in Ireland when the exodus started. Many thousands had left already going east and west to find a new home. If all had stayed home more than eleven million people would have lived on that breast of Brigit. The people who went early helped those they left behind to follow them to avoid the coming disaster. The home they left behind was ravaged by war and death, disease and starvation caused by the greed of the late arrivals.

Brigit became so tired from giving of her bounty only to see it sent across the sea for the profit of the few. My children went hungry. They starved. They lived off the sea and off the fruits of the greatly diminished forests, the mountains and the great deserts of bog and moor-land. They were punished for taking what I had prepared for them and had offered to them out of generosity and love. Many of my people were sent far away in punishment for feeding their families with the gifts of the land. This began the land-clearance campaign.

As the great forests were cleared to build ships and cultivate more profitable crops all of nature went out of balance. Only prudent husbandry could have sustained my growing family. But this was not to be. Brigit became sick and could give no more. Her breasts were dry and her bones rattled. Death and destruction roamed the land. My heroes had left to seek help from their cousins in Europe only to find there the same death and destruction in the older lands.

Two million of my people sailed west and east and south, to my neglected, older lands, in the hope of finding a new world, a new promised land like the one their parents remembered, a land of milk and honey, cornucopia. Another two million of my people died in coffin ships on the high seas on their voyages away from my island and were buried in the new lands, in the depths of the oceans and in the sickness of their minds and bodies. Some became lost and still roam this world and the Otherworld, weeping for what was lost, but knowing it can never return.

Those who were left on my island were a strange, demented people. They tore their hair and their clothes and cried to Brigit in their anguish. They felt forgotten, abandoned and turned their backs on me. *Is brónach an scéal é. [What a sad story.]*

But all people have their spring of youth and beauty, their summer of growth and plenty, their autumn of ease and rest. But the winter Cailleach comes every year to bring death and destruction. I had seen it all before, many times. Change comes unbidden and continues even when we stop looking. It has become more noticeable again in recent years.

This new Spring looks good. The wind is soft on my face and the rain is sweet in the fields. I hope for a great Summer. My children are mending their fences and repairing their tools. Brigit is stirring from her long sleep. She knuckles the sleep from her eyes and smiles at me. She is like her old self again, like Gealla with colour in her cheeks and the fullness in her figure. She is beautiful in the light of early Spring.

Bees search the heathers on the hills and the valley floors. Blossoms and flowers scent the air. A spotted trout makes circles in the pool of a mountain stream. The children are beginning to settle down. The Winter of war and turmoil is being left behind and the rite of Spring colours the sky and the future.

I am an eagle again. From the top of my high air lifts I can see forever. I can see my children's children coming home again to visit my island. They have not forgotten me. They cry when they step from the ships of the sea and air. They feel my spirit coming through the soles of their feet. They laugh as they walk my mountain paths and smile and feel at ease when they doze on the banks of my rivers.

They come from the land down under, with corks in their hats. They come from the coasts and great central plains of the new worlds. They are my children coming from the east again looking for the edge of the world. They are all my children, all the many millions of them, and they are all welcome.

Céad mile fáilte romhaibh go léir.
[A hundred thousand welcomes to you all.]

A Song of Tuan

I am Tuan,
I am legend,
I am memory turned to myth.

I am the path that circles the mountain,
I am the quartz on the hill of hopelessness.
I am the sparkle in a mountain pool,
I am a trout ring on the brimming lake.
I am the wind beneath the wing,
I am the heat in the rising air,
I am an artist. Who but I designs the swallows nest.
Who but I can crack the cuckold egg.

I am the grass on the far off hill,
I am the wink in the joyful eye.
I am the corner of the smiling mouth,
I am the wrinkle in the dimpled cheek.
I am the frown on the furrowed brow,
I am the flash in the angry glance,
I am the smell of summer flowers.
I am a fountain.
Who but I suckle the new-born lambs.
Who but I burst the buds in Spring.

I am the song of the soughing wind,
I am the rustle of the falling leaves.
I am the squeak of the cowering mouse,

A Song of Tuan

I am the crack of the breaking branch, overburdened
with snow.
I am the spit of the burning log,
I am the swing of a heavy axe.
I am the sting in the hammer handle.
I am song.
Who but I ring from the anvil strike,
Who but I give sleep to the nesting linnet.

I am Tuan,
I am legend,
I am memory turned to myth.
I will live forever.

Go mbeire muid beo ag an am seo arís!
[That we may live to see these times again!]

On Further Reflection

Again this story speaks for itself. The world is given many faces as Tuan, an ancient bard, changes to suit the new time, place and circumstance. Tuan is the voice of evolution, history and culture. As he or she has many faces, Tuan appears as many gods of the people or as the many faces of the one God. Typical of so many words in the Irish language the word god, *Dia*, has many meanings. To fully grasp the full meaning all possible meanings, like true wisdom, must be pooled.

8

FIONN, DIARMAIT AND GRANNIA

It was a day like no other. Although the sun was up it still felt cold. The frost of early morning seemed to hang on all day and Grannia felt cold in her bones in the depths of her cave even as she put more wood on the fire. But she knew why. Since midday, when the news broke that Fionn had been seen riding in his chariot in the hills above Glencar, she knew that this day would end badly. The view of Ben Bulben was obscured by a deep morning mist as she looked across the horseshoe valley of Gleniff towards the Annacoona cliffs.

Diarmait had been shifty all day. Although he still swore allegiance to Fionn he knew that Fionn had a long memory and an anger that could smoulder forever. He went about his ordinary duties preparing for the final hunt before winter sent the frosts and snows to devastate the countryside. They would return to Keash immediately if the hunt was successful. Every year the hunt was harder and seemed to finish later. The preparation was more tedious and more detailed than before and sent more splinters under his nail. He had more work to do on the antler tips to fit them to shafts. They made the best spearheads. Seasoning was all-important. But this year his head was sore and his concentration was at an all time low.

It was many years since he and Grannia had eloped. Fionn had turned the whole of the countryside upside-down in his hunt for them. Diarmait knew Fionn well enough to be worried even at this remove. You didn't run away with the promised wife of the leader of the Fianna, the greatest warrior in the world, and then sleep easily in your bed, ever. Now that Fionn was ageing his disposition was not as sunny as it used to be. He was duller company now and given to flashes of red anger and intolerance. A mean streak had come with the grey in his hair.

Although Fionn knew well that what had happened was truly not the fault of either Diarmait or Grannia, his pride would not leave him alone. On the outside all was sweetness and light but inside all was turmoil and rage, and he knew it. Even after all these years it rankled and left an acid taste in his mouth. It was no accident that he had come to the Shelly Place to hunt the Black Boar of the high plains. Ever since he had heard of the pair who lived in the high Palace on the Hill of Keash he was drawn there, inexorably, ineluctably, unavoidably.

He didn't know yet what would happen or how but he knew that, as sure as night follows day, the outcome would not be a happy one. Neither Grannia's *géis* nor Diarmait's love-spot

75

was an excuse or reason enough to a mind clouded by pain and jealousy. He had convinced himself that he had loved Grannia, not as he had loved Saba, of course, but somehow the loss of Saba was refreshed by the loss of Grannia. His nature was to flash, to strike out, to thunder and attack and nature comes through in all things.

Tagann an dúchas tré shúile an chait.
[Nature comes through the eye of the cat.]

It also bothered him that the greatest hunters in the world had not been able to find this young man, this friend that had been by his side on so many adventures and then had betrayed him. He held on to this story although he knew it was not true, but still it hurt where he hurt most. He had waited, moon after moon, for the scouting parties to bring him word of their whereabouts or capture and now, years later, he knew in his bones that this was where they were. This is where they had always been. And so he had to go, to resolve this old, thorny issue. What would this day bring?

He watched as Bran and Sceolán, his magical sons of the she-wolf, Tuireann, raced ahead, without a sound, without breaking a single twig as they flashed through the forest, heading for that grey limestone outcrop of Lug na Gall, the rock of the foreigners, at the foot of mountain of Gulbáin. The light was fading fast. Their late summer camp must be close by and he intended spending the night there. He had intended settling everything before sundown but it was too late for that now. He would have preferred to arrive earlier but fate had played its hand again, delaying them long enough to allow the light to fade and the gloaming to form. Old custom forbade the use of weapons after daylight finished. This imposed truce might give him time to clear his mind. This situation could not be easily resolved. Perhaps sleep would bring some flash of inspiration and relief from the throbbing pain in his head.

The protocols of hospitality had to be recognised. Fionn and his entourage were fed, bedded down and settled to sleep on the eastern side of the fire and the fire was smoored for the night. Fionn wanted sleep. He had an early start the next day to keep up his long established habit of a dawn hunt. But the mares of night would not come. The sky was black, no moon or star to lighten the darkness. On such nights the Pooka were about, and worse. He tried his left side, then his right side and then his left side again. He put a head under his knee but, no good. He tried lying on his mouth and nose but sleep continued to elude him and his mind was in turmoil. Bad thoughts came and haunted him, demons whispering of what he could do under cover of darkness. They were very persistent. Demons always are. He tried not to listen, not to pay attention, and he waited, waited for dawn and for resolution. It was a long time coming.

Grannia nodded off, in a fitful, restless drowse filled with dark shapes and eerie cold draughts that left her feet like stones. Ten bearskins could not warm her. This coldness was in her very soul.

'Diarmait, don't stir from our bed. Stay close to me. I've loved since I first saw you, love spot or no love spot. I loved you since we were children,' she cried out in her heart.

Political and war alliances were not the stuff of a young woman's dreams. How could men believe that duty came before love? It never did and it never could. These unsettling thoughts came between Grannia and her night's sleep. Diarmait slept easily. He had no disturbance in his mind. He was innocent of all wrong-doing. He had followed his heart and his *géis*, his responsibilities, even if they were not easy to do. He was at ease.

It came from the deepest, coldest shadows. It changed its shape with every mood swing, slinking and slouching toward the light of the campfire yet hating the light, all light, and all that went with it. It was drawn by the dark thoughts of Fionn and the frightened thoughts of Grannia. It growled with hate, spitting and hissing, round, red eyes glowering with rage. The very Earth trembled and shook as the huge beast cast around, looking for a path to the light and to its prey. It sounded like an underground river in full spate after the snows had melted. It smelled of putrid flesh and excrement.

Then it changed again and became a slavering dog, black and close to the ground, eyes aglow with anger and jealousy.

At length it took its final shape for this night, a shape decided long ago in the mind of Pure Evil. Tusks sprouted and its mouth lengthened. It shed its ears so as not to hear any reason. It shed its tail and with it its sense of balance. This creature had roamed this mountain waiting for this time to come. Ever since his foster-father had crushed his neck with his knees under the table in the great feasting hall at Tara it had waited for revenge. It careered through the undergrowth, snorting, spitting, hissing its hatred in blind fury and headed with unerring aim, straight to its destiny.

The furore in the woods woke the whole camp. Fierce hunting hounds whimpered and ran away. Grown men, hardened by battle and the relentless hunt, huddled in whispering groups not willing to make eye contact even with their best friends and soul mates. Fionn called for his dogs but none came. He looked across the fire to Diarmait for explanation of these strange noises and commotions coming from the woods.

Diarmait could not explain what was happening, even to himself, but his responsibility was clear. Whatever it was this was his camp and he must sort it out or lose the respect of his companions. No one offered to help. Somehow Fionn knew that this was the dark resolution he had hoped and prayed for. How would it resolve itself? He would wait and watch and see.

Grannia was up and dressed. This was Fionn's doing, whatever it was, it was Fionn's doing. She could smell it, feel it on her skin and it caused revulsion in the pit of her stomach. That screaming monster was the epitome of all that she had fled from: smothering duty, unquestioning loyalty and blind obedience to your elders and betters. It snarled up her gut and lit a fire in her head. She was engulfed with fear.

79

Diarmait, gentle as in all things, selected lighter weapons for the oncoming fight. Grannia implored him to take the *Gae Dearg*, the heavy war spear, not the lighter *Gae Bui* used for small game. Diarmait seemed to think that nothing too bad could be out there. Even when it was clear to all and sundry that something vile was on the move gentle Diarmait thought in terms of minimal response, least threat and understated action. Even so, he could not help but notice that nobody else was preparing to repel this Demon of the Night. They were following Fionn's lead, sitting and fidgeting by the fire and were glad to do so. Diarmait stood alone against the oncoming demon.

Then it came, screaming and roaring, making the bristles stand on its own black back and on everyone else's head. Diarmait pointed to the rowan tree refuge prepared long ago with Fionn's arrival in mind. He had planted two rowan or mountain ash trees years ago, one for him and one for Grannia. The two had grown together as they grew up. This was also his attempt to keep away any bad thing, demons or dark spirits that might come to visit. It had worked well until now. The dark side of Fionn was as bad as things could get.

Grannia climbed stiffly, twisted around and sat on a saddle-branch that joined the two trees to watch the coming battle with a mounting sense of catastrophe. The woods shook, leaves fell, the ground trembled and the night was split apart with heart-numbing shrieks and howls. All hell broke lose.

Gulbáin crashed into the campfire clearing, sweating, steaming, great gales of smoke in his nostrils and blood-red eyes burning all that fell in its glare. Without pausing he plunged at Diarmait. He had waited a lifetime for this moment. He could still feel and smell those strong legs clamp on his neck and the tightening, clamping grip, squeezing the very breath of life out of him, squeezing the very life out of him and he was filled with hate.

Diarmait's light spear, the *gae bui*, flashed from his right hand. Without a moment's delay the light battle-axe in his left hand flew to the target. Worse than useless, they only served to aggravate the already frothing anger of Gulbáin. Both weapons ricocheted into the dark wood having done no injury of any consequence.

Gulbáin's onslaught continued unabated as he tried to stampede over the waiting warrior. Only the swiftness and dexterity of Diarmait's salmon leap saved him. Gulbáin stopped and turned, raising clouds of stone and gravel, while Diarmait lay panting on the ground. The low-slung tusks sticking out from the black bespittled bristles came for Diarmait's chest and stomach. It was only a glancing blow but grave damage had been done. Blood and bone were bared. Diarmait rolled and ripped with his dagger even as the black mass of hate hit.

The squealing and shrieking increased until it was unbearable. Man and beast slashed and turned and struck out until blood and gore made standing difficult. On Gulbáin's final turn he eyed around to see a greatly weakened Diarmait in a kneeling position. This charge would surely be the last and lethal one. He had waited, longed for this moment. A ton of muscle, meanness and madness lunged forward. Diarmait had the best view possible right in the path of this black demon of the dark mountain. His body ached, beyond pain, beyond exhaustion, beyond thinking. Only instinct held.

The dagger in his hand was wet and slippery with his own and Gulbáin's blood. He could see the small, round, red eyes and slavering mouth as it came for him. He could smell the sweat and steam and the stench from the black and bloody body of the demon. The last thing he knew or felt was the wetness of that mouth as his dagger and arm went down the throat of the black mass of hate. Then the snout, tusks and great black brow of this mountain of evil exploded into his chest. All went dark; the demon, the surrounding forest and the light of life in Diarmait's eyes, all went black and deathly quiet.

His shattered body, with the last breath of life still in it, emerged from the darkness as the sun sent new light into Glencar. He lay under a crumpled carn of broken bones, blood and torn clothes. Although his eyes were open they were sightless. Diarmait had left this world but had not, as yet, reached the Otherworld. He could see his own limp body as he rose and floated above the scene of his death. He could see in great detail and with full understanding what was happening below, but he could not intrude anymore. The only thing he was unclear about was his own death. Was he really dead?

There was no sign of Gulbáin. He had disappeared back into the mountain leaving only a trail of blood and destruction up the side of the mountain. He was badly injured by the innocence of Diarmait, but he was as resilient as the mountain named and made for him. He would be available many more times to employ his fury and might in the black pursuit of hate.

The Fianna came back, sheepishly and shamefaced, to the spot from where they had abandoned Diarmait in his hour of need. Not one of them had raised a hand or voice and had certainly not lifted a weapon in his and their own defence, not even Fionn. In their flight and fright only their own safety and sense of security seemed to matter.

Fionn was last to arrive back coming in from the east. He crept in quietly almost unnoticed. No shout of the hunt or battle cry that morning. No morning chorus of joy and exhilaration. He didn't say a word. His silence was almost deafening. It made the whole world extremely quiet. He felt a mixture of embarrassment, shame and relief. He had failed his friend which, in Brehon law, was the poorest response possible. He didn't even try in any real way to help. His attempt was made disreputable by its degree of inadequacy. His face was down-cast. It was covered by a cloud of self- disdain and derision.

Grannia was white-faced, pale, as she examined and straightened Diarmait's body or what was left of it. She told Fionn where there was water, clean, fresh spring well-water that was so pure that from the druid hands of Fionn could cure Diarmait, even at this late stage. She could tell from the cold look in Fionn's eyes that it was a vain hope that depended on his good will. Three times he brought the water of life in his cupped hands. Twice he fumbled it, spilling it on the bare rocks of the mountain trail.

On the third attempt he made it to the side of his dying friend and rival in love. Too late! All hope declined and descended into the abyss of a deep depression. The mortal life of Diarmait had ended as Fionn, with his empty gesture, hovered over him. It was Grannia's wail that filled the void. It shook the very foundations of the world. It was emptied of all faith, hope and charity. It was filled to overflowing with despair. Fionn turned red, white and blue in the face. His embarrassment was all-consuming.

No more would Diarmait roam the hills on the hunt for the bounty of the Mother or sit beside Grannia by the campfire at dusk singing songs and telling stories of the hunt. No more would he range the morning fields and woods in search for game and experience. From now on he would be the source, the well-spring of many stories around the fires of his people until time itself runs out and the world stops turning. His reputation for gentleness and good will would remain for a long time while all others would be remembered for the inadequacy of their response to his needs.

Grannia's heart was broken; her soul was loosened from its roots. The love of her life was gone. No more would he warm her with his sunny smile and disposition. Her life now had no purpose, no centre, no meaning and no reason to continue. It would not continue for very long.

Fionn and the Fianna left the camp early next morning as the sun came up. They headed west towards the sea at the edge of the world. They did not dare go back to Tara. The story of Lug na Gall had raced there on the wind and their shame and embarrassment prevented them from facing their own people. Some say that Fionn was never seen again around Tara or Émáin Macha, Almu or at Naas na Ri. Some say he was seen at Crúacháin, head down, his fading locks matted and uncombed, a spent man.

In time he made his way overland to the sea, out beyond the ninth wave, from the west coast of the Shelly Place, sailing for Hy Brassil following the sun to its night home. And when the sun had set he sank, for the last time, as a deeply depressed man into the darkening ocean. In dying he gave his life's blood to the sea and the sky so that even today we have great red sunsets in the west, lighting up the Shelley Place and the approach to Hy Brassil, the Isle of the Blest.

Many years later the local people found Fionn's bones washed up on the shore at Cumeen strand. They carried these bones to Carrowmore, An Ceathrú Mór, and buried them at the focal point of the sacred nemeton site and raised a great carn over them. This heap of stones marked the end of an era for the Fianna and for the people and for the world we once knew.

Others say that he finished his life looking for Saba in the hills above Glencar. And some say that he is still up there and can be heard each morning at dawn following Bran and

Sceolán as they race together through the forest on the never-ending hunt. The story of Fionn, Diarmait and Grannia lives on in the memory of the people. Now you know it.

On Further Reflection

Grannia is the constant dilemma, dichotomy or contradiction: a shape-changer; a waxing and waning moon; full of love and hope; madness and despair. Diarmait is the rising sun, full of innocence and hope, not strong or worldly enough to see the cold reality of Dark Menace. His 'salmon leap' marks him as the shaman, the wise man who cannot see violence as a solution to any problem. He is the person who can make the intuitive leap into another cultural viewpoint.

Diarmait and Grannia live in caves, the wombs or bowels of the Mother, and come out only to hunt. The sun never shines in the Otherworld of their cave. They are creatures of the Otherworld who leap into reality only when something extraordinary happens, in this case, the death of the sun. Hermits and monks, seers and *saoi* and the three sisters of the Cailleach often live in caves.

Fionn is the setting sun, empty of faith, hope and goodwill, the aging or failed warrior. The Fianna remind us that even the greatest warriors need a leader of courage and deep integrity. War is not an end in itself, only the last option to achieve a worthwhile community goal. They teach us of the need for faith, hope and charity, the very foundations of friendship and the needs of community where all are considered equal in every respect.

In many stories we find the three faces or phases of the year exposed as people: the Spring of youth, the Summer of active years and the Autumn of content old age. Some call them the

'Three Faces of the Goddess'. Three faces or phases refer to the structure of creation: birth, life and retirement in modern terms. The number three is ubiquitous appearing in triads of rhyme reason in many guises. We find three faces of the god: the prepubescent, the active and the wise or experienced face. But each face has a counterpoint in its philosophy: the naive youth, the destructive warrior and the foolish old person. This story make the three faces of the good clear: The juvenile face of Grannia; the combatant face of Diarmait, and the post-hunting face of Fionn.

What is missing is the face of Winter when everything in creation dies. It is not part of creation but something different. It is the face or phase of death, the leaving of this world and going to the Otherworld. The fourth face or phase can be seen as one of evil if death or the opposite of creation is considered evil. In this case it is one of evil represented in this story as the black boar. People with this mindset saw creation as worthwhile and valuable but saw death as an end of goodness. They had no concept of an afterlife. At best they saw transmigration of the soul or rebirth as the next possible good thing. Life in all its glory was what was valued.

9

NIAMH OF THE GOLDEN LOCKS

Niamh thoughtfully brushed her hair and gazed at the clouds from her window high up in her tower. The wind was silently blowing to the east and the land of the little people. She could see forever from here. As she had done so many times before she wondered what it might be like there. She had heard so often about these small people, small in stature and small in ideas. They obviously needed help. Even their chief, Fionn, seemed so weak and wanton in comparison to the men of Hy Brassil, those tall, imposing giants of the western world who held the world in place, controlled the winds, moved mountains and who, each night, shepherded the stars towards their resting and rising place.

What if she could catch one of these mortals, and train him, train him in the ways of her world, perhaps he could then be sent back to the world of the little people and improve their lot immensely. They needed help, that much was clear. This would be a challenge worthy of her talents and her time! Time? She had plenty of it. It meant nothing here where Fionn's Fianna were mere characters in a story. Time was a product of small minds involved with small ideas.

The horses were already in the field waiting with the wind at their back. The time was ripe. She would put her plan into action. She chose Caoilte as her mount, big as a house and as strong as a hurricane coming out of the west. The other horses would follow to cover her trail and for company on her trek. They headed east to find this Sacred Isle of the Blest, land of heroes and little people. Only clouds showed on the horizon with the sun somewhere behind them. She would get there as the bright ring of morning encircled the sky and their world became awake again. Nobody slept in her world.

The Fianna hunted the western glens at this time of the year, as they have done each year for as long as anyone could remember. Fionn favoured the high plains above Glencar for the great stags and wild boar that roamed there. He spent the moons of autumn in the Shelly Place each year. He liked to hunt there with a small and select band of warriors and this year would be no exception, though it would be different.

As Caoilte rounded the brow of the last prominence Knock na Rae rose from the waves, standing at attention, on sentry duty above the shore. Niamh nudged him with her knees to follow the course of the ancient river that led to the old village in the valley among the hills. His snorting raised great clouds to disguise their entry to the Land of the Little People. Cumeen strand was coming into view where she could bring him ashore to dry land. He stood there for a while in that liminal space between water and shore, prancing on the water line and sniffing the air. The salt felt good in his nostrils. He shook his long flowing mane and signalled for the other white horses to wait for him and his precious load by the shore, lapping the waters. His golden shoes would keep him from touching dry land but he had to pick his way with great care. If he stumbled, and Niamh should touch the ground, all would be lost, his mission, his honour and the beautiful Niamh of the Golden Locks would dissolve into a vapour that might never make its way back to Tir na nOg, the Land of Youth and Promise.

The estuary narrowed and the *crom leachs*, curved stones, appeared to their right on the brow of the hills above the river. Crossing the lake brought them to the hazel wood and on to Lug na Gall. Niamh could smell the heathers and grasses from the meadows high above the lake at Largy. There, still, lay the open court tombs of the Fir Bolg, centuries after the Fir Bolg had left and retreated to their home in the east, far beyond the Grey Door. In the distance, towards the Glen of Aodh, the music of hunt and hound sang out through the early morning air. The Fianna were on the trail.

Bran and Sceolán had raced soundlessly, with the first beams of sunlight through the thickets, trailing a magnificent stag. This majestic beast had led them a merry chase all through the dawn. Now it was slowing down and the hounds were gaining ground. Fionn was close behind on his favourite hunting chariot. This dawn chorus burst through the mountain copses and undergrowth screaming and shouting in excitement and exhilaration and charging recklessly. The entire retinue sang loud while it spread throughout the countryside bringing the world awake.

Oisin had dogged the chariot all night. He had raised this stag. His own fairy nature had sensed the beast, hidden in the thick brush and, without being aware of it, he himself had roused this relative of his mother, Saba, sooner than good hunting practice decreed. He knew that the chase would be exhilarating, the race joyful, before the stag would escape into the high cover above Glen Aodh. In this way he satisfied his split allegiance to his Fianna comrades and Cernunus, Stag Lord of the Forest.

Fionn had sought Saba, high and low, in these same foothills. Saba, the beautiful Danaan woman, the great love of his life, had been taken away from her home at Almu by Gollan, the Dark Lord of the North and father of Balor. Gollan intended that she would be his consort in his crystal castle under the waves. She had shape-changed, to take the form of a doe to hide amid the great deer clan of this valley, intending to escape from Gollan. Saba and Oisin had been brought through here on their way north. That soaked and sodden land was still recovering from the onslaught of the Formorians.

Saba had left Oisin playing in the grasslands for Fionn to find him while she followed the Dark Lord through the rainy woods of Largy. She had still hoped to make good her own escape but could not risk the recapture of her beloved son. When Fionn found Oisin he had been playing with the fawns of Largy at the edge of the forest in the early morning sunshine.

Oisin knew these woodlands like he knew the back of his own hands. He knew more than anyone that the fun was in the chase, the glorious chase, when the blood ran red in the veins and the mind floated above the menial details of life. This journey of flight and fancy was the stuff of dreams of young people since the world was new. The way of the hunt was supreme.

As expected, the running stag finally turned, doubled back on his own tracks and ran for the shore of the lake of Aodh. With one mighty leap from a prominent crag near the crannog it launched itself into the shining waters of the lake. The mighty beast put both distance and height between himself and the baying hounds. He was safe now. His leap put him out of their reach, for today at least. The hunt would wait for another day.

Oisin stood on the cliffs above and watched him swim to the far shore. He threw back his head and laughed at the swirling dogs and hunters, milling about on the outcrop below him. Swiftly, he turned on his heel and strode back into the woods, straight into the eyes of Niamh of the Golden Locks. She had come out of the forest and just sat there staring at him. She sat there, on her enormous white steed, a wondrous vision beyond all understanding.

As he drew up short, his surprise showing clearly, Oisin gaped as this beautiful woman reined in her panting mount among the yelping dogs. They waited for the hunters to gather in a large circle about them in the early morning sunlight. The hounds finally settled while the warriors found soft ground to rest on. Protocols were observed as required when two clans met. Fionn came forward to greet the unexpected arrival. With his two favourite dogs, like light and shadow at his heels, Fionn strode from the edge of the clearing and addressed Niamh. He enquired of her mission. He knew that she had a mission; she would not be here otherwise.

Her eye had already settled on Oisin and although she conversed with Fionn her attention was on Oisin, son of Saba, the mystical fairy princess, and of Fionn, sunny chief of the Fianna. Oisin would come with her; of that there was no doubt. He had stood there, like a big bostoon of a boy, open-mouthed and speechless since she had first arrived. He was not even aware of the conversation going on around and about him, concerning his life and future. Proposals were put and discussed and decisions reached somewhere above his head. His mind did not interfere or offer any suggestions.

His one and only thought was of how soon he could ride away with this fairy woman. He said yes to everything: yes, yes, yes; including that he would go with her to Hy Brassil and would learn whatever she wanted to teach him and do whatever she wanted him to do. Somehow he felt that he would teach her a thing or two as well. Men! Would they ever wake up?

As if in a dream he mounted the steed behind her and with his arms embracing her he took the reins. The Fianna cheered them as he swung the rearing horse with the golden hooves towards the west. The great hooves flashed in the sun, sending blinding darts of light into the eyes of the Fianna, preventing them from seeing clearly what was happening. All this happened in a daze. Fionn was concerned for Oisin's welfare but what could he do? This young man was smitten, in love, besotted beyond all rhyme or reason. Logic and common sense were out of bounds. What could any man do?

Oisin was away with the fairies. He was totally immersed in the moment. His breath came in deep gasps of astonishment and wonder. The past was gone, a far country, while a future had not yet occurred to him. And now he was mounted and on his way, to where and what he did not know. And he was delighted to be going! With a final snort, the great beast cleared his nostrils of any reality, whirled his golden hooves in the air and was gone.

The sun was high now as they rode the bright road to the west. It was all a blur for Oisin, like the fluttering of bird's wings. He was dazzled by the beauty of Niamh, the smell of her hair and the music of her voice, like the singing of mountain streams of a spring morning. The energetic beast moved easily beneath them. The plains of Largy flashed by and were soon left behind. The sea was calling, calling in that relentless and brooding roar that sounded like rolling thunder in the distance.

The beast seemed to grow beneath them as it gathered itself for the long journey ahead. Its mane flew and shook in the freshening breeze. His tail was up and his flank muscles rippled like the tide on the long strand at Cumeen. The fresh salt air in his nostrils gave him the energy to make the run to the sea, the shining sea, sparkling in the sunlight on the horizon. The enchanted threesome came down from the brow of Gulbain's hill and headed for the *rós*, the headland point directly ahead.

Strange! The sun was setting early today. Time had shifted. Long shadows made the brow furrows of Ben Gulben frown as if worried by the outcome of this pending adventure. A great warp in the continuum had taken place. The Otherworld had broken through. The thin veneer of reality had rippled and cracked. Oisin was becoming more aware. In the half dark he could hear animals calling in the distance, at the edges of his mind. A Great Stag whistled from the cliffs at Mullaghmore and was answered by a nickering doe from the foot of Knock na Rae. The Black Boar of the Mountain himself was abroad, snuffling and snorting in the sedge along the shore of the Glen Car waters. A sea eagle skree-ed from the heights above Drumcliff, Druim Cliabh, the Ridge of the Rush Bundles. It soared to a great height and had a clear vision, all the way to the ocean. Magic was afoot and the Pooka were abroad in the hills.

The pair on the magnificent charger skimmed the waters of the bay, passing Cumeen, where they had come ashore, heading for the fiery point on the horizon. Tir na nÓg, where time stood still and its people stayed forever young, lay directly ahead. The other sea horses that had waited for them near Cumeen strand joined them and they churned the trail to froth, riding across the sky to the sea on a milky white trail of foam.

As they passed the seventh wave a great shoal of salmon smolt surfaced and swam along with them. The gleam of their silver bellies winked on and off as they turned and rolled through the curling waves. Their bright, unblinking eyes scanned the pair on horseback, eyeing each other and the striding, prancing mare of the deep. Oisin could sense them speak to each other and he understood what they were saying to him. Questions flew, of destiny and causes, and the why of things flashed through his mind. The simple answers of these creatures of the eternal waters seemed so clear and complete and uncomplicated.

These anadromous creatures knew it all. They had received instructions from the Mother of All, as they travelled from her womb through her life channel to the sea that held all the wisdom of the ages, everything ever known, since the world began. They had been swimming in this sea of wisdom for so long that it had soaked into their very being. With a signal from their leader, and in unison, they all swung about, taking a new heading and moving swiftly towards the *rós* now far behind them.

As the ninth wave came and passed by a monster of the deep surged to the surface and surfed ahead to show them the way to Tir na nÓg. The crust of shell and shingle of ages past along the line of his back seemed to point the way to the future, a future that for Oisin was so full of promise and joy. The leviathan smoothed the way until the sun set and then continued in a white stream of foam until a light appeared out of the blackness. No moon lit the way or showed the trail to follow. Only instinct, the guide light of the Mother could bring you to that point of light. Like the star of morning, the light on the brink of eternity set a true course for them. Suddenly there were there.

Golden gates opened as they approached and music, soft and sweet, filled the air. The bounding beast beneath them became smaller and strutted to a halt on a mossy green or bawn in front of a large castle that was made of glass and gold and silver. Everything glinted and glittered like salt on a fresh fish. A stream of people, all laughing and talking came out to meet and greet Niamh and her new catch. What would she think of next? Her enchantment with the people from beyond the eastern horizon had been noted long ago.

The young man with her looked bright and doe-eyed, like a grilse in spring, strong in body and clear of mind. He talked freely and answered all their questions and had many of his own. The group moved back into the castle and wined and dined through the night and the following day and on into the next magical night. Food was never brought to the table. It was there in abundance no matter how many people came or went. The conversation was unrelenting, the singing was magical, the music lifting the heart and keeping the soul in tune with the spirit.

Oisin laughed his way through the milieu and met with everyone who came to share his stories and to share theirs with him. It seemed to go on forever, a timeless, seamless flowing of joy and companionship and 'the craic was mighty' as they say in the Shelly Place. He didn't feel tired or weary of this university of life. Brehon laws, good hunting and tracking, fairness in the division of the spoils of the hunt were all up for debate and review. The lives of fish, birds and animals seemed an open book to these people who discussed the finer points with an enthusiasm and intensity that was the foundation of all learning and true wisdom.

Oisin couldn't help but notice how the dress and hairstyles of his new-found friends reminded him of feathers and scales, fins and furs. Had they spent so long on the hunt that they had begun to take on the character of their prey? Had they amalgamated with their quarry? Had the division between human and animal, fish and flesh, dissolved in this salty environment? This intensive engagement had brought all the kingdoms together. Academic separations had melted in the heat of intense conversation. Oisin felt the knowledge become part of him, soaking into him, in his hair, in his blood and in his bones.

And then, it changed. His perceptions blurred, his mind clouded. It became misty. After an eternity of immersion in this wonderland, the mist gathered before his eyes. All those around Oisin began to shape-shift. First they became amorphous, then transparent and then they melted into the mist and floated away from his knowing. He could feel a breeze rising, full of sounds and smells that reminded him of home. Home? The idea seemed foreign to his mind but somehow he felt that he must go there. A distant drum called to him, beating incessantly, fast and demanding and calling him back from the depths of his mind.

It was morning when Oisin's head cleared again. He thought that it must have been the wine. But all his oceanic friends were gone. The sun was up, high over Largy Plains, and a soft breeze rippled through the grasses and ferns. Where were Fionn and the Fianna, and had that stag made the far shore safely? His bones were stiff and his body felt heavy. He must have slept for a long time. He could hear a hunt that was far off but the whole world seemed cooler and less tangible. This long beard that reached his belt was grey and thin. The hair on his head felt thin and light and the backs of his hands looked strange to him, wrinkled and mottled and yellow-brown. What kind of dream had come in the vision of Niamh? This fairy woman had worked her magic well. He felt the weight of great years on him and wisdom beyond all understanding.

He would go into the world and see what he could tell his people of the wonderful sights that he had seen. What would they think of what he would tell them of his adventure? It would take a long time to recount it all and for them to understand all he had been given. Would he see Niamh again or was she just a figment of his imagination created from his hunger for knowledge? He would seek out Fionn and his friends and discuss the whole thing with them. They would help him to understand all that he had come to know and help him settle his mind. Wouldn't they? Well, wouldn't they?

On Further Reflection

For me, this is the greatest story in the Sligo landscape. It bridges the gap between the real and the Otherworld, the world of

Spirit. Sligo has been described as a thin place where the veil between the two worlds tears very easily. For me, it breaks through when I am walking through the landscape. So many times I have felt my mouth open in awe at the magnificence and absolute majesty all about me. I begin to feel light-headed, a little unbalanced or giddy and unless I ground myself with something to eat I can have an out-of-body experience.

The experience of shifting, the altered state of consciousness, is what the story is about. It can be achieved in many ways but its purpose is to transcend the everyday world and to enter the world of Spirit. It is a spiritual experience. Many anthropologists and philosophers have written about this phenomenon, but the experience must be allowed to speak for itself. I have seen other people moved in the same way as me. It requires only an openness of mind, an eye for beauty and a spirit of curiosity.

The shamans of many traditions used this effect to travel to the Otherworld to seek answers to questions of great concern to their people. Oisin's journey tells in a very clear way what the experience is like. He was a shaman that sought wisdom for his own people. Michael Harner wrote about this work, *The Way of the Shaman* (Harper and Row) and made it clear that travelling on the drum, the rattle or on the breath was common practice throughout the world.

St Patrick and Oisin talked about the nature of the life experience. In many ways Christianity in Ireland was built on the pre-Christian traditions and found much in common with them. The spiritual experience is missing from much of religious practice today. Those who seek it often turn to alternative and complementary versions of health care.

10

THE BEGINNING OF THINGS

High on the Hill of the Moon, Knock na Rae, stands the carn of the Great Mother. She stands there, in all her magnificence, viewing all in creation, her creation. She watches as her children come into the world, play the game of life and then return to her. This is what she intended since she first thought of creating a world of her imagination and inherent mystery.

Across the valley, on the Hill of Carns, stands the mound of the Great Father. He stood with the Mother since her first thought echoed in his mind, a vibration at the beginning of the work of creation. The first thought began a circle of gifting that sent the Mother and Father into orbit around each other. Every thought that has passed between them since then has orbited with them to produce time and the space for the world and the cosmos to form.

Thought is the act of creation by evoking a response. Word allows thought to enter the world, an expression vibrating and moving out from its source. This produces enough space to enable the world to form and evolve towards its climax. All thoughts, words and deeds are children of evolution. Time and space confines and supports them as they inhabit the Mother's brooding bubble of imagination. The early children of Brí inhabited in the valley of the Shelly place, in Sligeach, Sligo. This was not always so.

In the beginning was the *cúinneas*, the quiet. Nothing moved or slept. Nothing hunted or swam. There was only dead quietness, total silence, the *cúinneas*. The Great Power in the universe liked the quiet. It was so pleasant and peaceful. It was such a great luxury that it seemed unbecoming to keep it a private experience and better to share it – but with whom? The hushed Power pondered this situation.

The mothering part of the Power wanted to fill the *cúinneas* and held out for a good decision. The fathering part wanted the *cúinneas* left intact. It was too beautiful, too elegant to disturb. He kept his head down, became introverted and held his council. She continued to intercede for change and fulfilment. The gap opening between them created space. Time began while they waited for the tension between them to resolve itself. The tension first formed two mounds and later, when filled with the wishes of the Mother, it created the landscape of the Shelly Place.

The mounds faced each other across the void and felt lonely. They could see each other but could not touch. They could hear each other but could not speak. They wished to be together again in time and space. The lonely tears of the Mother dropped into the void between. The Father became concerned and made a valley to hold these precious tears. Nothing of the Mother could be lost or wasted. The valley held as many tears as it could but, eventually, it overflowed. This overflowing surge symbolised the love and generosity of the Mother, Cornucopia.

The valley represented the strong supporting cup of the Father. The cup overflowed and so the Father made a great cauldron to hold this sea of tears. The salty tears crystallised in the warmth of their new love and made little shells of the pure white. The Father set mountains around the waters to further contain and protect them. These stalwart guards became green with envy at the beauty of the sparkling waters and drew up the pure, crystal clear liquid and sprinkled it on the hillsides.

Trees sprung up to cover the envious outcrops where some water trickled through their clumsy fingers. Leaves from the trees gifted themselves back to the waters to make amends for the theft. In time they fished themselves down the river to the sea. Some leaves fluttered in the air and hovered above the water until they flew, as birds on the wind, above the new and flowing river.

The Mother and Father looked at what had begun and smiled. The Father's smile formed a ring of joy around his face and it shone brightly giving life through its early light. The Mother's gentle smile lit up the deep frowning shadows cast by the mountains and sprinkled the crags with stars that grew as flowers. The sun of the Father and the moon of the Mother chased each other across the sky and around the mountains in a game of love, life and creation.

In time the sun grew to be a great warrior, a leader of the frowning mountain Fianna while the moon became a Druid, storing all the wisdom of creation in the river of life of their new world. They debated the best way to organise this new world. They exchanged views as they coursed across the sky on their daily journey, watching the developing environment below. In time the Druid prevailed in the debate and triumphed over the Warrior. She was often seen to eclipse him in dialogue. Creation, filled with the sound of the dawn chorus of the new world, became a habit for the landscape to wear. Quiet agreement became the rule of life. Reason and good sense overcame any wish to war and strife. Cooperation proved more powerful and productive that competition.

The Druid took the Warrior apart, dismembering him and putting every part of him to good use in building the world. She used his bones to make more rocks and stones, his blood to make more water and liquids, his flesh to make clay and soil to cover the bareness of the mountain slopes and the valley between them. This gave the world a richness that altered forever the course of the landscape. The thoughts of the Warrior were used to make clouds to clothe the sun and the moon and to distribute water to all corners of the valley.

And so the Great Power created the universe, by considering it, meditating on it, discussing, remembering and reviewing it. In time, Earth's children grew to take an active role, a Warrior's role in assisting the Druid Mother. Together they enriched the valley, the surrounding mountains and the river that ran to the sea. Each child was given a special task, a good reason for being in the world and a means of continuing the process of evolution.

The children became diverse, developing new trajectories and enriching themselves with the wisdom of experience. Nothing was overlooked or forgotten. Each child had a unique contribution to make. Each task was carefully selected to match the talents of each child. Each one became part of the thinking that created the world. They became of one mind.

You too were made in the same mind. You too are never forgotten.

On Further Reflection

This is an Irish version of a creation myth. There are other versions but this is my favourite one. Nobody ever spoke to me about a creation myth set in Ireland. In fact, many academics say there are none, but I put this version together from bits and pieces of comments I heard from local people. It attempts to explain the unknown and, perhaps, unknowable.

11

MYTH AND LANDSCAPE

Sligo is encircled by carn structures on the peaks of the mountains that surround it. The town is held in the arms of the Mother and guarded by her warrior sons. The carns of stones are made from the shield-stones of warriors who survived in battle and the carn was the lasting reminder of the battle. Shield-stones were placed in the bottom crease of a hide shield to give it weight and stability when it was hit by a weapon, and to give it momentum when it was used to strike an opponent.

Méasgáin Maebh is on the west side of Sligo, on top of Knock na Rae. Maebh had many battles but this carn commemorated her battle, as Brí, with Gollan and Balor, the Dark Lords of the Formorians. This battle is often associated with

Lugh, the Sun God but it was Maebh's protection that was at stake. The hot sun drove away the frozen waste brought by the Formorians. The warrior was defending the Mother.

Maebh in story is set in Bronze Age times and tells of her as a warrior Queen of Connaght, the western province of Conn, her predecessor and son of Nial Naoi Giallioch, or Niall of the Nine Fosterings. Fostering was a way of strengthening alliances between neighbouring clans. They swapped children to ensure that hostilities would break out between them only as a last resort. The more fostered children in a clan the higher the prestige as they represented many alliances. The number nine was a form of infinity and seen as the boundary of the count. Later, unkind writers translated the word *giallioch* from the Irish as hostage, an unfriendly, war-like and irresponsible term.

Maebh is the symbol of the responsibility of the chieftain and the female aspect of nature. Mother Nature, Earth Mother and Great Mother are names applied to Maebh in her earlier mythic story. The name Maebh translates as 'passionate' or 'intoxicating', and was an old Irish word for ale which was used as part of the ceremony in the inauguration of chieftains.

Maebh and mead are related. This is explained as the intoxication of the warrior – her blood lust, in defending tribe and territory – but also as the intoxication of the mother in protecting her young. A woman defending her children was the most ferocious force imaginable. The great warriors, Fionn and Cú Chulain in particular, were trained by women. The name Maebh was brought by the Celts from the common culture of Europe and its Indo-European ancestors.

In Ireland the earlier names of the Earth Mother were probably Brí, Brigit, Danu, Doni or the Mór Riaghain, depending on which period and which group of people were in power at the time. Brí and Brigit, the bright-faced one, was also associated with the Moon and Wells. This coincides with the early meaning of Knock na Rae, the Hill of the Moon. The carn is often referred to as Measgáin Maebh, Maebh's 'lump of butter'. Wells were the exit from and entry to the body of the Mother and a way into the Otherworld. The shaman's journey was often envisaged as starting by leaping into a well.

The Ox Mountains to the south have carns on their many peaks to mark the southern boundary of Sligo. These are some of the oldest carns in Ireland, with an archaeological date of 7,700 years ago on Crúacháin, the high peak above the White Door of Ladies Brae, or way of passage through the line of hills.

Carrowkeel, the Narrow Quarter, with about thirty carns on top, is at the eastern edge of the county at the end of the Ox

Mountains. This is the site to which the early people migrated when Carrowmore became too small to feed its expanding population. By this time, 700 years after the arrivals came from the sky and sea, the climate had changed. The temperature had dropped by 2° centigrade on average and the climate changed from sub-tropical, with good growth all year 'round, and seasons, as we know them today, had developed. The structures at Carrowkeel face the turning cosmos and mark the rising and setting sun, moon and major constellations.

The Hill of Keash, on the southeastern horizon of Sligo, has a large carn called the Principal on its skyline. Stories of Fionn McCumhal, Cormac Mac Art and other characters abound on this mountain. My favourite story set here was of the Cailleach, the old woman bringing her cow home at dusk. The cow bolted into a cave on Keash and in she went after it. She caught it by the tail and ran after it through the underground caverns all night. At dawn she and the cow emerged at Crúacháin, near Tulsk, twenty mile to the south. They emerged through the 'Gates of Hell', the way out of the Cave of the Cats that contains many stories.

Carns Hill is on the eastern horizon of Sligo with Romera's carn on top of it. As we saw earlier, Romera was the older warrior that killed Oghamra, the young lover of Gealla who lived on the islands of Lough Gill that is named for her. This story seems to be an update of an earlier story of Fionnabhair, Fraoch and the Dark Worm of the lake. The theme of these stories is common in world mythology and is repeated in many Sligo and other Irish myths. The central theme reflects the story of the Rising Sun, the young man, the Setting Sun, the older man, and the Moon, the girl of the stories.

Romera is the name of a local warrior chieftain in a story set in Bronze Age times and was developed to explain the carns in Roman Christian times. Daghda of the older creation story was rendered as Romera: he was roman-ised. The earlier mythic story is of Eochaigh Oll-Athair, the Dagda Mór or Bilé, the male god of the same people who named Maebh on the opposite side of the valley. The earliest name was Bilé who was the Sky Father. The Sky Father was the mate of Brí, the Earth Mother.

Brí and Bile gave birth to twins, an Grian, the Sun, and an Geallach, the Moon. One grew up to be a Druid and the other grew up to be a Warrior. In time, the Druid overcame the Warrior; common sense overcame the will to resolve difficult issues through war. This is symbolised by the eclipse of the Sun by the Moon and is retold in *Táin Bó Cúilgne* as the Brown Bull overcoming the White Bull. The Druid dismembered the Warrior and used the bones to make the mountains, the flesh to make the earth, the blood to make the watercourses and his thoughts to make the clouds.

The Dartry Mountains to the southwest have carns that form a continuous line of carns on the Sligo skyline. Dartry derives from *Dartra*, the old Irish name for the red deer, and gave rise to the English word to dart or darting, from the creature's ability to slip in and out of the forest at great speed. This range of mountain carns connects on the skyline from Knock na Ré to the Hill of Carns. This skyline set of marks told all entering Sligo from land or sea that people were already settled here and proper protocols must be followed to ensure safe passage. Sligo was the great door between north and south and between sea and land. Sligo was a place to live and a door-way city, a destination and a way through.

111

On Further Reflection

Sligo is a magical place, a place of myth, mystery and imagination. It is also a good place to live and in which to rear children. I lived in many countries abroad and in many places in Ireland but, in some way, I never really left Sligo. My heart and soul remained here and, like the stones, they will always be here.

12

THE CLIMB TO MAEBH'S CARN

McGlynn was at it again. The weekend had hardly begun and already he was at it, waving his arms about and singing in that tortured and broken boy-soprano voice. It was quite ridiculous at the best of times but from a forty-year-old scoutmaster? Words cannot begin to describe the pain that it inflicted, and on an early Saturday morning? Too much entirely! At least the weather was up and looked promising for the weekend camp. Summer Saturdays always meant weekend camping.

Destination: Outer Culeera. The Fairy Glen would be base camp and from there the troop of nine scouts, two leaders and a scoutmaster, all seasoned warriors, and eight cubs, warriors in waiting, could spread out and sweep the peninsula clear of all invaders, especially Brownies and Girl Guides. Thoughts of them, with their skirts and berets, sent a cold shiver of dread from head to toe of this otherwise daring band. The image was horrendous.

But we would have to be careful. We felt *her* eye upon us even before we topped the hill at the sports grounds and headed past the last of the houses and into the wilds of the Culeera Peninsula.

She, Maebh, the warrior queen! Why did it have to be a woman on the mountaintop? Why not a real warrior, like Finn McCool or Cuchulainn? Why some awful woman for those awful Brownies and Guides to crow about? So unfair! And all the old stories that McGlynn told us was of a woman who did the advanced training of all the great warriors, just to add insult to injury. It was Scóta who had trained Cúchullain at her camp in the far north. The only explanation for this terrible dilemma came when I saw my own mother getting really mad when a bigger boy picked on me and she let him know, in no uncertain manner, that he had better watch his step. That was very scary.

The Fairy Glen seemed a long way off but we didn't think too much about that. 'Hike like a sheep' was the policy in getting there: just one step at a time. The rucksacks got heavier as the morning wore on. The relief of just putting them down raised the humour of this band of prepubescent warriors as they struggled out of their rattling pots and pans that hung from straps and strings. Fires were lit straight away. You can't have a camp without a campfire – basic boy scout lore. And so the weekend fire festival began. This fire was stoked endlessly with broken wood until we broke camp on Sunday evening. Tents went up and billycans were filled and put on to boil.

Later we would figure out what to boil in them but first the protocols had to be observed – fireplace, fire, boiling billy can, tent – the basic essentials.

I occupied my favourite spot under the big elm tree close to the trail leading to the well and waterfall. We went to collect the broken timbers that recent storms had left strewn on the ground, like broken limbs of giant warriors left on a battlefield, and stacked them near our fireplaces. The old stone rings from earlier fireplaces were tidied and cleared of ash. We had built our own from the stones left behind by those earlier wandering bands of boy scouts. How old were these rings of stone? Nobody seemed to know. The scouts had been coming here for more than thirty years. But maybe they were there from ancient times? They were so like miniatures of the great rings of stone on the plain above the glen at Carrowmore. If so, there were thousands of years of fires to cook at and be warmed at and to sing around. Our camp made us part of it, this ancient tradition, or so we thought.

This thought brought another stirring of the unconscious as would happen so many times on such a weekend. The challenge of a visit to that mysterious place on the plane above the glen brought the temperature down a degree or two. We mustn't think too much about it. Time enough for that later. We would survive it again this year but it still caused a chill. Maebh looked down in stolid silence.

We were in a hurry to get out of the Glen. All that shelter and shade and chill was not good for you, especially when there was a white sea roiling around on the beach just two hundred racing steps away. Swimming togs and other essential items of clothing were strewn about the tents and the roar of the warriors competed with the roar of the sea. A cool splash of froth and foam soon obliterated all threats that the stone circles or Maebh might hold.

She was always there though, looking over her shoulder, observing all actions taken by our frolicking troop. Sticking your head under the surface as you swam towards the shore gave some protection from her stare but she was always there.

Sitting on the shore trying to dry off with a sand-filled towel was a painful and useless exercise. It was made worse by the presence of all those seashells packed tight on their shelves along the shore since time began. 'Kitchen Middens' McGlynn had called them when he tried to educate us in the way of the Ancients. Who were these strange people? Where did they come from? What were they doing here? Who could know? Certainly not McGlynn! He was much too ordinary to understand the workings of the magical powers that stacked these shells so neatly. Mustn't delay here! Best get away and quickly before something weird would happen. The campfire brought warmth and removed some of the chill brought on by the Atlantic rollers and the presence of the Ancients.

McGlynn was in boss mode and was rallying his troops. Hike to Carrowmore? Go straight into the gates of hell? The young cubs thought it a terrific idea. Must be the small brains in those small heads that they had? Incapable of critical thought and this meant that they would follow McGlynn to their doom. Sad really! Great warriors could be lost before they would ever taste the sweet wine of victory and all because of recklessness by McGlynn. Such is the way of scoutmasters. But, if we had to go, it was best to put a brave face on it, and may God help us and deliver us from evil. Amen!

The rolling grassland of Carrowmore can be seen from a long way off. It is about five kilometres from the sea to where the landscape is dotted with those strange *crom lechs*, curves in stone. All those stone circles and circles with dolmen centres and stand alone dolmens are big enough for a whole troop to dance around in. The stones themselves are tall enough to give shelter from the cool breezes that swagger around the low hills on their way from the Atlantic. They can be cold and strong enough, even in high summer, to cut through even the heavy material of scout shirts and go up the legs of short pants. Goose bumps arrive on that wind and with them the thoughts of what savagery those pagans could have been up to long ago. We only had dark thoughts about such rituals. What is strange or different is usually frightening to the untutored mind.

McGlynn was not of this variety of course, or so he thought. He maintained there were celebrations for bringing children into the world, growing up for the boys to become a hunter or for the girls to become a mother, forming a hearth and getting

117

old, past hunting and childbearing, as well as dying to be re-born. Chieftains were acclaimed here, as were the gifted people of the clan who could do wonderful things with their tools, and were hosted and feasted. McGlynn said something about burning bones and putting dead bodies out for the animals and birds to pick clean. Ugggh! The very idea made me shiver.

And who knows what else. McGlynn didn't know everything. All sorts of other terrible things could have happened here: maybe the killing of young boys; young lads who had done no wrong but to be born on the wrong day or at the wrong time? That was possible. Killing for the sake of killing! These stones must have run red with blood, great gollops of it dripping on to the grass and forming pools between.

And then burning them, even before they were fully dead? Oh God! I could hear the screams of those young warriors and felt that I could be next. Imagination took flight and ran riot. That huge stone box in the middle of the field! What did they do there? Half-dead bodies stacked waiting to be burned? What dark satanic ritual could have fitted into that box? What awful memories and stories did it contain? Such thoughts ran wild in fertile young imaginations and, although totally unfounded, brought blind panic to the brink of consciousness.

No wonder we were scared of the thing. Who in his right mind would want to go inside of it? But that was the very thing we contemplated, the challenge that we faced each year. Who had the courage to climb down into the hollow, cold and damp blackness and sit there? Watching and waiting, for minutes that seemed like hours, waiting for those black, hairy monsters with slavering mouths and red raging eyes that would surely come if the door to the Otherworld should open. If we survived that ordeal we still had to climb out of it, even when semi-paralysed with fright and cramps. The run, at full tilt away from this accursed place before some lightning bolt coming from the black and threatening sky would come to obliterate every particle of your being was the final test. You were a real warrior and man after you did this, but never before. This was the supreme achievement for a cub wanting to become a real scout and for a young Sligo boy wishing to grow up.

Maebh waited for us. Her carn was on the mountain-top but some said that she was in the mountain. She had always witnessed the awful things that had occurred at Carrowmore and seemed to approve. She marked for life all those who dared such deeds and numbered them among her warriors. Such warriors were suited to the tasks that *she* would set out for us. Only her chosen ones could guard her carn and repair any damage done to it by marauding scoundrels from Ballisodare or other foreign parts more than five miles away from Sligo town.

The ritual path leading to the centre of the complex at Carrowmore was another challenge. What beings would come out of the ground or out of the air if the pilgrimage were not done with proper respect? This ancient labyrinth had been walked by many for millennia before now and held the aura of things blessed and strange about it. Even cubs would walk it. They had no proper realisation of what could go wrong. Spiralling in to the great stone box was best done in early morning when the sun was rising. Spiralling out was best done in the evening when the sun was setting. This made it a day-long ritual, with sandwiches and red lemonade at high noon.

No one had ever actually seen any of these spectres that could arrive on such a soul journey but we all knew that they were there. Once you entered the portals of the spiral near the Clock Well and began the route, you were fair game for a fright. Sitting on top of the main feature was an experience that left a lasting impression on young minds and young bums. Yet, to court disaster in this way was what growing up was all about. No wimps were tolerated. Dare or die was the motto. Some of us nearly did die – of fright. Like the time McGowan and Foley went to enter the great dolmen, site 7, that forms one of the portals to the labyrinth, only to be confronted by a horned demon coming up from under the Earth. The fact that it was a white faced bullock with uncut horns was lost on the pair of runners. They took off over the horizon in the direction of Sligo town, not to be seen again until the next scout meeting, two weeks later.

Saturday night at the campfire always followed the same ritual. The enormous heap of logs and *cippeens* were stacked to the side of each campfire and fed incessantly into the gaping maw of the fireplace. Burning warrior limbs seemed a suitable thing to do for a band of wandering mercenaries. Eating of semi-raw food and drinking liquids that could easily be taken for blood in the half dark gave feelings of the primitive mind and altered states of consciousness. Tingling sunburn or the damp shirt, wet from the late evening rain shower before the fire was stacked high, enhanced this feeling.

The howling of the older warriors, faces painted with mud and powdered paints, frightened the cubs and caused them to huddle together. When they were sufficiently bonded they would begin their own howling and screeching to rival the falsetto and breaking tones of the older group. Songs were attempted early in the night but midnight required stronger magic. The wolves, bears and wild boar that circled the campsite had to be kept at bay. Wild and dark magic was required for this. This was when the howling began in earnest.

The girl guides in the lower valley could be heard singing silly convent songs, no use at all for such rituals. Tra-la-la-la's and fol-de-rols were no good in fighting demons. Our chorus was intended to strike fear and trepidation into hearts and souls. Did girls have souls? Was it possible that these lithesome, winsome creatures could be considered equal in some way with fearsome warriors? Could they merit consideration for a place in the mystery of the Otherworld? Did they experience any of the altered states of mind or were such states merited only by warriors? But what about Maebh?

Maebh on the mountain gave great cause for concern. Was it possible that a mere woman could have led the warriors of Connaght against the most feared warriors of all time? Who had won that battle anyway? Ferdia was killed. Cúchullain was killed. A bedraggled Maebh came home without the Bull of Cúiligne. Red Branch warriors fought their comrades and laid waste the corps of stalwarts from north and west, and all for the sake of a woman's vanity? Surely this was all the fault of those who put a woman in charge of warriors? Such questions rolled around in the heads of our band of young and aspiring warriors as we contemplated the climb that lay ahead of us the next morning. Much preparation was necessary to ensure that muscle and nerve were steeled and taut enough for the trek to the summit. Tomorrow!

Early Mass at Strandhill church helped to alleviate the guilt feelings left over from the heathen orgy of eating and burning, mental plundering and pillaging of the night before. Now we were ready for the main task of the weekend. The climb to Maebh's Carn was not hard to do if you went up the eastern face of the mountain where the gentle rise of the trail was not too demanding. Even girls could manage this route. But this was not a suitable track for aspiring warriors. We went up the ancient fairy path, up the precipitous southern face with its un-ending steps-of-stairs approach to the summit. They seemed like countless steps, ledges that obscured the next ledge, until you finally crested the hilltop directly above the Fairy Glen, the hosting place of the *sidhe* and the scouts.

McGlynn again issued the challenge and the cubs re-sponded so well that you had to admire their total innocence and be amazed at their total credulity. The older, case-hardened scouts could not afford to demur. Perspiration trick-led down the small of my back and dripped from my forehead as we ascended the mountain. Every sinew and muscle was strained to the limit under a scorching sun and a fierce deter-mination, born of the fear not to fail in front of the whole as-sembly, in this push for the summit. We could not fail and we did not fail. When the heights had been scaled, the task of returning the disturbed rocks to the carn was demanded by ancient writ, going back at least to when McGlynn was a new scoutmaster. This fifteen-year period, to a time before most of us were born, had given rise to many of the life- and limb-threatening rituals that now ruled our lives each summer.

Circling the carn sun-wise gave no clue to its contents, no more than the assault to its summit did. Neither the standing stones on the north–south axis nor the smaller carns out along this line gave any clue either. McGlynn said that the woman herself was in there, under this enormous pile of stones, standing upright, in full battle dress, facing her enemies in the north. Who could they have been? The Ulster tribes were her family, through her marriage to that wimp, Ailill. He couldn't handle her and seemed to be more her servant than her husband.

I heard my mother say once that it wasn't Maebh that was there at all. She had been told by my father's mother that it was the same woman who was in Lough Gill and the river, the Garbh O'C or Garavogue. Some Mother of all creation was there. Wonder who she was and what kind of husband she had? Hope that he was better than Ailill. This more ancient husband was supposed to be in the big carn above the lake and the father of Gealla, the Lady of the Lake. All these people were set into the landscape and nobody sure of who they were. Very strange! Bringing a small stone up to put on Maebh's Carn had been done by the locals since God was a boy. We did it too, every time.

It was on the mountain trails that we would meet the dreaded girl guides with a *streal* of brownies strung out behind them. Anger was the instant response to such trespass, and confusion. This was Maebh's mountain and the Guides taunted us with this. They claimed precedence in rights to be on the mountain, but we argued that warriors took precedence in all cases. We had no basis for this except that we felt that we had the power and strength to impose this decision.

The Guides, on the other hand, could assert without the power to impose. We had them there. Didn't we? If it ever would come to open warfare we knew that we would win. Men always won. It was ordained to be that way. By whom? By warriors, of course.

And so the ancient betrayal by the warriors of the people that they were set up to protect was played out again and again on the side of the mountain. Men were supposed to protect women, children and the elderly. This was their *geis* or self-imposed task from earliest times. But that had changed when hunters became warriors and they lost their sense of duty. As a result, things had changed for the worse. Just passing each other on the mountain trail raised animosity that was blamed on our hormones. Nobody seemed to know how our hormones got this message in the first place. It was one of those mysteries of life not yet resolved.

Coming back down the mountain was easier. We came down the eastern trail as it was faster. We didn't complete the ancient trail. That would be tempting fate too much. We short-circuited the route to Carrowmore as we had done that bit the day before, but we knew that that was the wrong order of things. No one knew why we had altered it. It was probably McGlynn's idea of being proper Christians or some other modern concern. Warriors were not too worried about these things until the demons came near and then we became very Christian in our prayers.

The very idea of food, available at the campsite, gave speed to tired legs. The final snack, anything edible left in the rucksack, was supplemented with whatever you could take from the rocks on the seashore; some dulisk, cockles and mussels with the odd oyster, if we were lucky. We had an expression about the freshness of such seafood. It was not thought fresh enough unless you could hear it scream as it went down your throat.

The taste of salt is in my mouth even today and reminds me still of those boyhood days of wonder. Maebh was all pervasive, omnipresent and omnipotent, omnivorous. She was the greatest mystery in our young lives. She drew many thoughts to young minds that have not yet been resolved. She tested and trained warriors for life. She was our warrior queen and gave a meaning to our lives that neither philosophy nor religion could match. Most of all she gave us the gift of awe. This opened our mouths and our lives to so much more. She was like our Mother. More than fifty years later, she still is.

On Further Reflection

I was born in Sligo. My home, which overlooked the Garavogue River, was at the edge of Sligo Town within walking distance of all the major mythological and archaeological sites. I walked to all of them before I knew what they were or who put them there or why they did so.

I passed a large fairy fort on my way to and from school every day of my young life. Maebh's Carn and Carns Hill were in sight of my home and afforded places to roam and play as a boy. This sparked a lifelong interest in the mystery and mythos of these sites that was fanned to flame by the conversations overheard in the everyday speech of family and friends. This flame still burns brightly. I invite you to take a spark and bring your own fire aflame.

During my working life I visited over 35 countries. My delight in the stories of other people added to my own enthusiasm and led me to read Joseph Campbell's books comparing the myths and legends of many countries. I was disappointed to find that Campbell had not included Gaelic, Celtic or Irish myths in his anthropological works. This work is still waiting to be done. I have started the Sligo Myths and Legends Summer School as the first step towards this work.

Campbell and others brought the discipline of anthropology to my attention. This led me to a course of study at the National University of Ireland at Maynooth to complete a BA (Hons), an MA and a PhD in Cultural Anthropology.

In many ways, the landscape of Sligo shaped my life, my values and belief systems. It informed me and formed a foundation to build a life on.

Would you like to explore this landscape? Join the Sligo Myths and Legends Summer School and explore to your heart's content. Enjoy the stories, the sites and the excitement of the journey.

13

Passing on the Gifts

Gealla had enjoyed a long and busy life. It was more than sixty summers since her birthing by her mother, Brigit Bán, who was the principle healer, *the bean feasa*, to her community. Brigit's gifts gave her high status in the clan and were appreciated by those of other communities who lived nearby and had benefited from them. Bones were rejoined, bruises were soothed and pain was alleviated even when no physical injury was evident. Brigit cared for body, mind, soul and community.

The knowledge included in-depth details of vegetation – plants, flowers, grasses and trees – and of all the components of human and animal bodies – skin, glands, stomach, lungs, bones and flesh. Knowledge of the mind – memory, imagination, instinct, emotions, feelings and pain – was deeply debated and digested but, most importantly, knowledge of soul and spirit as it existed in each individual and community was gathered and explored. The whole person was considered when healing was needed. This holistic form of healing consisted of curing of physical ailments, while caring was targeted at their affects on mind, soul, spirit and community.

Her knowledge and wisdom were legendary and needed conserving and continuance. How could this be done? Those gifts had transferred to Gealla when she was still in her mother's womb by a means that reflected the understandings of life, soul and spirit held by her community. Gealla had added to them from her own experience and by sharing with other healers in the local and extended clan system. In time, Gealla passed the gifts to her first daughter, Fionnabhair, the current community healer, and to her son Omi, who now lived with a nearby clan as their healer, their *fear feasa*.

How were gifts transmitted from one generation to another? How could the contents of a mind be transferred intact? How did soul, spirit and community bear on this transfer? Let me tell you how Gealla received her gifts from Brigit Bán and her grandmothers before that.

Brigit was recognised as a great healer when still a young woman. Her mother was already principal healer even before Gealla was born, and this gave Gealla the opportunity to learn and practice the art of healing from a very early age. But she too had inherited her gifts from her grandmother, Brí, a woman she had never met and knew only in her bones. When Brí was at her peak in mid-life, aged about twenty-five summers, her grandmother had given her a leather bag with a small, perfectly round stone in it, along with some ochre, to wear around her neck. This stone and bag had been handed down from grandmother to mother to granddaughter for many generations.

Brí had worn the neck-piece for the rest of her life with her soul soaking into the stone as the vigour of her step diminished and the power of her mind overflowed into the stone. This hard sphere already held the over-soul or great spirit of the earlier generations, and the sum of all knowledge and experience gathered during the life and death experience of each healer that had worn it.

As Brí lost mobility and spent more time near the hearth teaching her grandchildren, the stone's power strengthened and grew. When she finally became weak and close to the time of passing the iconic soul-stone was kept in direct contact with her so that all her soul was collected and contained.

When Brí did pass her body was blessed by her daughter, Brigit, now principle healer, who covered the body in ochre and curled it into the foetal position. The body was then carried to the carn of stones on sacred ground on a hill near the clan hearth.

The birds and small animals came to consume and dismember the body, to fragment it and spread it throughout the district.

One month later Brí's people collected the major bones that remained, broke them to expose the marrow and release another layer of Brí's soul to the stone that was kept close to the body all that time. A fire was lit and the bones were burned and Bri's soul was finally fully released from the bone-fire to gather in the soul-stone.

The neck-bag was then placed on Brigit's neck so that when Gealla was conceived Brí's soul was transferred ready to be re-birthed, re-membered with all gifts included, when she was born. Not only was Brí re-birthed and remembered, but parts of the over-soul of all her earlier generations were re-birthed with her. Gealla had generations of knowledge and experience in her bones right from birth. She had the memories.

On Further Reflection

The talents in a family often skip a generation! So I was told when I was very small. The story you have just read helps to explain this thinking. There is some truth in the idea. Children often look for a role different to that of their parents so as to reveal their individual selves.

A child is often predisposed to a particular way of life or to develop a particular talent by being told that 'you are just like your grandfather; he was very stubborn also'. This sets up a set of expectations that can determine what you do with your future.

Or, when you grow up in a house full of music, song, dance and stories is it surprising that you like to play music, sing and dance, and to tell stories? I can vouch for the truth of this. We filled our lives in a way that radio and TV now does in modern times, but I think we had more fun. We entertained ourselves and each other.

14

THE CARN AT KNOCK NA RAE

I grew up in Sligo in the 1940s and 50s. It was a wonderful place in every sense. The lake, river and sea dominated my active childish world but, more than anywhere else, Knoc na Rea dominated the landscape. That strange and awesome carn on top of this mountain affected my life in many different ways, each way that gave meaning to the carn, the time it was built and the people who built it.

The stories about the carn stretch over a period of 5,000 years. In my lifetime, Maebh was entombed in the carn and every so often, as much as five times each year, I would hike, sheep-like, up the mountain and walk, sun-wise, around her carn three times before doing the final push to the top. On every occasion I was agape with awe at its size and the colossal effort spent in building it. The huge igneous kerbstones are not native to the limestone mountain and were taken up from the lowlands. How this was done is still a mystery. The limestone fill material was excavated from the top of the mountain on the seaward side of the summit, all 50,000 tons of it.

The shape of the carn gave it one of its names: Measgain Mebh. It is roof-shaped, the same shape as a pat of butter formed with the small wooden paddles I saw in use in my Aunt Lily's kitchen when butter was being churned. Another name, Miosagain Mebh, suggests that the moon is involved somehow, *miosa* being the Irish word for month. This also fits in with a possible meaning for Cnoc na Rae – the hill of the moon. I like the coincidence but do recognise that there are many other possibilities.

Rae or *ré* is a tough word to translate. One Irish-English dictionary gives seven different meanings for *ré*, and if the truth be known, all of these meanings contribute to the full and original understanding of the word. Who can know after so many millennia of use?

The Book of Ballymote calls the mountain Cnoc na riabach, 'the hill of the hostings'. This is the oldest recording of the name which gives it some weight, but it is lightened by its close connection with the Christian churches. The writers may have been involved in re-naming and re-meaning the sites associated with the pre-Christian period. The deliberate project of mystifying, confusing and general cover-up of the earlier belief systems was well under way in early Christian times, and it persists even today.

That St. Patrick drove the snakes out of Ireland is the best example of this baffling of the truth. The snakes were the druids of course. The poet William Butler Yeats kept a hosting connection alive in his poem, 'The Hosting of the Sídhe', where he says 'the host is riding from Knocknarea'. As one friend asked, who were they and why would they host on the top of a mountain? The only people who 'hosted' there when I was a child were the local boy scouts. We would camp in the Fairy Glen at the foot of the mountain and climb the back of the mountain early in the morning and host around the carn. We went there to visit Maebh, of course.

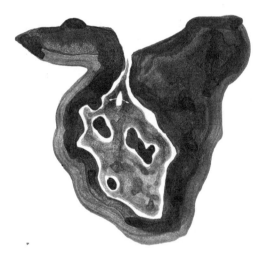

But who is this Maebh who we went on pilgrimage to see? She is said to be, in local lore, buried in full battle dress facing her enemies in the north. Her husband by marriage was from the north. He was Ailleach of the Gríanán on the mountain near Letterkenny, out on the Derry road. Maebh and Ailleach are characters in many stories that are set somewhere between 300 BC and 300 AD, the stories thus being around 2,000 years old.

The story I heard as a child when being put to bed was that Maebh was the queen of Connaght, the western province of wisdom. The story about the Brown Bull was her attempt to establish the place of wisdom in the sorting out of disputes without going to war. War was associated with the north, commerce with the east, while music, song and dance were associated with the south. A good chieftain needed competence in all these aspects of life in order to be selected and sustained as chieftain.

But let's get back to the mountain. The problem is that the carn has been dated by its type to be in excess of 5,000 years old. I do not know of any dating done from materials taken from the carn by archaeologists. It has not been excavated, and probably won't ever be. It is made of loose and broken rock and is not suitable for tunnelling. Also, many local people would be very annoyed, including me, if there was ever an attempt to interfere with the carn. 'Leave the magic alone,' I say.

So, who was there, and why, for nearly 3,000 years before Maebh's time? We can never know for sure. As I said, 'Leave the magic alone'.

The story I like best tells us that Brí was there. She was the old Earth Mother, the cauldron of plenty: cornucopia. Her husband, the Sky God, was called An Dagda Mór at a later time. He is buried on top of Carn's Hill, on the opposite side of Sligo to Maebh's mountain. Maybe you can tell me his earlier name.

Dagda and Maebh had two children: the Sun and the Moon, a boy and a girl. One grew up to be a warrior and the other a druid. In time, the druid overcame the warrior and used his body to make the Earth – the bones to make the mountains, the blood to make the watercourses, the flesh to make the soil and the thoughts to make the clouds. This gives us a creation myth set into the Sligo landscape. Some scholars tell me there is none in the Irish tradition.

Maebh had three 'faces'. Gealla was the young virgin set in Lough Gill. Maebh overlooked the sea and was the warrior woman who shed her blood in giving birth. And Maebh is also in the sea, the storehouse of wisdom. Her long legs stretch from the fording place at Sligo town to Strandhill on one side and Rosses Point on the other side of Sligo Bay. The Garbh Och resides in the Garavogue river that is the path between the womb of the lake and the place of wisdom and death in the sea. All rivers die in the sea.

These stories are being lost to the people of Sligo. The selection of Yeats and Benbulben as local icons has added to the detritus that has covered them up. By all means honour these new icons of more recent vintage, but please, not at the expense of losing our more ancient heritage.

What I have related here is a small part of this more ancient heritage. It is forgotten by many, but not by all. It helped to shape my life and taught me to consider what life and the world is about. It can do the same for you if you will allow it.

On Further Reflection

This story explains itself. It is at the root of many other stories. They weave through each other and form a web of mystery to catch a passing child.

15

ACQUIRING WISDOM

C ian was perplexed. He was already a man of fourteen years and it was high time he had decided what he would do with his life. Would he be a warrior or a druid? Would he choose manly and gallant violence as a way of life or would he go the way of the scholar and become a reclusive *saoi*, shaman or wise man? He felt the need to do something worthy with his life but could not decide, could not know which life he would make. Warriors defended their people from attacks of hostile foreigners and invaders while druids defended their people from hostile foreign spirits that might invade the mind or the body of their people.

All the iconic figures of his childhood were gone, unavailable to him, to guide him, to show him the way, to advise him, to instruct him and help him discover his true calling and to nurture his vocation. His father, Oscar, a well-known warrior, a man-in-arms, had been killed in war when Cian was still a babe-in-arms. Oscar's mutilated body was burned on the funeral pyres of the battlefield and never came home. His mother was so distraught that she could not take care of him and he had gone to live with his wise grandparents. They were old and stiff and confined to the hearth, but they did take good care of him until he was twelve years old.

In a very short space of time both had died in the hard winter of two years before but not before they had inspired him to follow the way of the druid, the shaman, the wise person who guided the people in their everyday decisions: when to plant, when to kill or trade cattle, who to listen to for advice and where to build a new hearth. This had been the work of Damhlaig, his grandfather, and Tegan, his grandmother. He grew up strong in mind and body. But now what was he to do with himself? Would he follow his father to war or his grandfather to battle with demons? Either way he was in for a fight. How would he know what he was supposed to do?

His father had followed the Fianna in the ways of war but now the Fianna were all dead or gone. The seven arts of warfare had fallen into disuse. All was bloodshed now. Fionn, a one-time leader of the Fianna, the greatest band of warriors the world had ever known, was moping about somewhere in the north west in a greatly diminished and depressed state. He had behaved so badly in his dealings with Diarmait and Gráinne that he had dishonoured himself, so much so that he could not come home to Dún Aillaine in Kildare or to Tara in Midhe.

Rumour had it that he had sailed into the western sea and did something drastic. That was the first night the sea had turned red at sunset.

Oisin, once the happiest man in the world, was away with the fairies. He was last seen riding on a great, white, golden-hoofed stallion, behind a beautiful golden-haired fairy woman, on his way to Hy Brassil, the land beyond the ninth wave. He was gone so long now that Cian had only vague and jumbled stories of him. Oisin could be of no help to him now.

What was the matter with these men? Why were they behaving in such strange ways and leaving Cian to fend for himself? How could they do that? Why were they not here now? Who would prepare him for all that life promised and threatened? Abandoned and forgotten, a little sad and lonely, that's how he felt. He was stuck in a liminal place, a time warp and could see no way out.

Cian's grandfather had followed Dian Cecht, the great healer and follower of Daghda, the god of all knowledge and Goibniu, the smith that made the world. All these were gone too but not entirely forgotten. But they were not here now when he needed them. Everything they knew and everything they could do was now in memory only. Grandfather Damhlaig and Grandmother Tegan had told him stories about them but what can ancient story do to help a young man in the modern world. He had heard some story about a man far to the east that was wise, could do great magic and was open to help people.

Some say that he had been killed by the elders of his people because he, like Socrates the Greek, was a threat to them. They didn't like threats so they had removed him. However, at present, even if he were still alive he was too far away to be of help. But he did give Cian the idea of being of service to his people. Not to be a *gillie* or mere servant boy to run errands, but to be a servant on the grand scale: heroic, brave, handsome and famous. That sounded about right for Cian.

Wait a minute! What had Grandfather Damhlaig told him about getting advice from those who had gone before us and were now in the land of spirit? It was something about sitting in meditation and ritual practice, travelling to the Otherworld to find a guide. There were ways to do this if he had the courage and resolve. What had Grandfather said?

He could starve himself until his mind wandered away to meet the Spirit and ask the hard question. Starvation! No thanks! Or he could try bloating himself with hot food and soups until he fell into a weakness and met the Spirit. Sounded a bit better but where could he get that much food together and someone to help him. No! Not that way either!

He could find a cave somewhere up in the hills and wait there, without anything to disturb his senses until he lost his senses and met the Spirit. That could be possible. He knew a cave high in the hills above the lake. Maybe that would do? Hold on now. That cave was the night home of some brown bears and a million bats. Might be quiet during the day, but at night things could get very exciting, too exciting maybe. He would spend the hours holding his breath, afraid to make a sound and certainly not eating anything, but there was a good chance that he would end up as breakfast for the bears.

He could wait until he was badly injured in battle and suffer the pains and aches of recovery and being maimed with a bad leg wound. He could spend years relearning to walk. Or learn to hear what he could no longer see, if he had a head injury that blinded him. Or he could spend years learning to swallow gruel and soups if he got a bad neck or chest injury. Cian didn't like the sound of any of these options. Learning wisdom was a costly business but a man could over-do it, try too hard and maybe still not become too wise.

He would learn about herbs and roots, rites and rituals and become famous. He would make potions and poultices and sing the world back to health and happiness. This is what his grandmother had done. She had been in training for more than twenty years and then still had to keep learning. All that adult education! A man could only take so much learning without doing himself an injury. Prolonged study and learning! I don't think so.

How else could he do it? There must be a better way. Oh yes. Wait a minute. Yes, he remembered now. Both grandfather and grandmother had told him about the fast route to wisdom. Something to do with hazel nuts! It was late summer and the hazel nut trees were laden down with nuts. He would sit under a hazel nut tree, wait quietly until a nut fell into the river and then he would drink the water filled with the bubbles from the falling nut. Sounded a bit strange but he thought he could do it. How hard could it be?

Cian walked along the river bank until he found a suitable hazel nut tree over-hanging the river and got himself comfortable underneath it. He waited an hour and then some. He waited, and waited, and waited. Would a nut never fall? A small stick prodded his backside and a fly buzzed in circles around his head. He paid no attention. Soon enough it got dark but the moonlight encouraged him to sit still another while, and another while, and another while. It was cold and he felt hungry but he remained calm and disregarded the discomfort.

He sat there quietly and considered everything that had brought him to this nut tree, to sit under it. He thought about his predecessors and all that they had done, both good and bad. He thought about what life offered him, all his parents and grandparents had done so that he could have the luxury of sitting there contemplating life and death issues. He had plenty of time to think. The thinking distracted from the stick in his bum and the flies around his head. Nuts fell but he missed them. He was too late to get their bubbles.

Three days later it happened. A nut fell into the water just in front of him. He nearly missed it. He was hungry, tired and jaded and full of river water. When he saw it fall he jumped to get his jug into the water scooping it up without bursting its bubbles and managed to capture the targeted water, bubbles and all. He got the jug to his mouth and felt the water and bursting bubbles go down his throat. He had done it. He got back onto the bank and waited. He wanted to see if he felt any wiser. He didn't feel any different. Did it work? He would have to be patient to see what great insight would come. Eventually, it did.

Although he didn't feel any different he realised that he had sat for long enough and thought deeply enough to learn that he could sit there for such a long time and think deeply. This insight, this piece of wisdom, the product of a sore bottom, itchy head, rumbling stomach, full bladder and a busy mind, convinced him he could try to become a wise person, just like his grandparents. Whew! What a relief! Job done!

He would spend time, twenty-one years in all, with the wise people of his clan, learn the signs and symbols, spend time in the star-chambers to travel to the Otherworld, and he would instruct the young men and women about how to be successful in life. He would be there for them, always. He would not abandon them, would not forget them and leave them alone or lonely. This was his true calling. He would answer that call.

On Further Reflection

How do we decide what to do with the life we have been given? Our parents, relatives and friends can influence us but our ancestors have laid the foundations. They broaden and yet limit our choices.

In hard times we appear to have little choice and are glad to do what we can to make a life. In good time we can have the luxury of deciding what it is that suits or satisfies us best. Later in life we can makes changes, sometimes radical choices, and change how we career around our planet. Even then we need people who can look at our life and give us an opinion on what to do next or about a given situation. We call these people friends and we are lucky if we have friends who are wise and caring. Without such friends we can become lost in our own smaller world.

16

THE WISE WARRIOR

Tegan was eighteen years old. She had married Liam two years earlier but he was dead now. So was her son, Eoin. Both had died when their home was attacked by renegade vandals looking for loot and booty. They had found little enough as the family was too young to have accumulated a lot of wealth and their predecessors had not engaged in the accumulation of wealth. They had lived in a communal way, sharing everything they had so that nobody went hungry or was left without a place to live. All were organised to take care of the weakest and most vulnerable.

The most vulnerable were the women carrying children in their wombs, very young children and very old and disabled people. If pregnant women did not survive the clan would not survive. If the children were not protected the clan would not survive. If the old were not protected their knowledge and wisdom would be lost and the clan would be greatly weakened without them.

A new way of living had arrived in recent years. It had arrived with all the babies and new people from over the waves. The population of the area had grown and resources were less easy to get to than before. There was tough competition for the needs of living. The hunters needed to stay closer to home to protect the hearth from bandits. This further reduced the food supply and imposed more dependence on locally gathered supplies of vegetable and fruit. Thankfully, the sea was close by and fish was plentiful, but the hunters–turned– warriors had to stay close to ensure the catch was not taken on the way back to camp. Even so, much of the sea supply was seasonal, especially the seashell food.

The practice of some hunters staying at home to guard the hearth diminished the number available to roam the landscape looking for game. The idea of clearing a large number of trees of leaves to let the sun shine through had developed. This was done by taking a ring of bark from around the base of the tree, starving the tree of sap. Nobody was sure how this started but now the clan could not have survived without this technique. The sun reaching the forest floor allowed fresh grass and vegetation to grow. The area was usually cleared around a small well, stream or turlough lake. The stream was most useful as it gave greater accessibility to the long rush of water. Hunters could sit at the edge of the nematon area and wait for deer or boar or game birds to arrive. This was best at sun-rise, sunset and at high noon when it was hot and dry.

The Great Mother, who supplied all that was needed – animal, vegetable and water – was most generous and most needed at these times. Eventually, when the trees rotted and fell they were heaped into a pile to clear the ground further but, in time, this heap became a shrine to the Mother to recognise her generosity. She gave of her bounty to help her people to survive and thrive. Her lesser creatures – animals and vegetables – were sacrificed for the greater good. The people felt the need to thank her, to use her gifts wisely and to ensure that they did not become depleted. They worked with her to ensure their survival as well as their own.

The battle for survival was fought within rules of engagement. Protocols were developed and followed conscientiously. If an animal was taken it was necessary to make best use of the meat, bone, hide and entrails. If a tree was felled it was necessary to plant two more in its place. If berries were taken it was necessary to feed a berry bush with the waste from the hearth after food preparation and cooking. Wood ash helped the green vegetation to thrive.

But Tegan now felt that all that was behind her. The world had shown her that family life was not for her and that she must find another way to live. She was strong, healthy and agile in her body, even if her mind was deeply hurt. Most of all she was angry. She wanted to strike out at those who had brought her such hurt but she knew that she would never be sure just who they were. She had been away at the sea coast and came home to find the devastating scene. Many others were equally hurt in that attack. She joined with a few of them to train as warriors, as people who made war a lifestyle, whose role in the community was to be proficient at defending the hearths and deterring attackers. It was also their intention that, in future, if any renegade group did attack any local hearth that punishment would be meted out to them by the warrior band. They would soon learn that there were consequences to attacking a hearth in this area.

Defending against renegade human groups was treated as dealing with marauding groups of animals. Much the same tools and techniques could be applied to track, surround, attack and chasten any retreating band or to send out the message that it was unwise to attack any hearth in the locality. Most of the weapons were developments of farming tools. What could be applied to soil, crops, trees, foxes, wolves or to hunt rabbits could be turned to warrior use with great effect. What could cut the head of a stalk of corn could, with a little weight added, cut the head from a man or woman.

Tegan favoured the slingshot. It was light to carry, could be tucked away out of sight until needed and then employed to great effect. A round pebble shot from it could raise a fine lump on a man's rear end, take a man down if applied to the knees or legs while a well-selected, well-directed stone to the head could be fatal.

An early task was to mark out the territory so that the warning was clear to anyone crossing the boundary: from here on be careful, courteous and move through quickly. This territory is already taken for our use. The piles of stones were Tegan's idea. They represented the stones that might fly from her sling. They also had an older message. They represented the decision making events where local laws were agreed. All those voting for the final decision placed a stone in a pile and the biggest pile won the day. Those encountering the piles of stone knew that they had a decision to make: behave or expect trouble.

In time they also came to represent the piles of stabilising stones taken from the bottom of the hide-covered shields of fallen warriors after a battle. The stones became so much a symbol for warrior craft that in time they were thought to contain the soul of the warrior. This was suggested by the old creation story where the bones of the warrior were used by the druid to make the mountains that surrounded the Shelly Place. As with all symbols, each one had many meanings. For Tegan, they symbolised the hard facts of life:

If you harm any hearth be prepared to pay retribution.

She took great satisfaction from this. It helped to cool the anger of her own torment. They removed a weight from her mind. Her slingshot became a tool to heal her soul. She saw the flying stone as a soul flying into and out of this world just as the wise people saw the birds. The blackbird was the soul of the shaman. The hawk was the soul of the warrior. The red-breasted robin was the soul of a friend or neighbour.

In time Tegan became established as a great warrior. She shed her own and her tormentors' blood in settling disputes and disagreements and in repelling invasions. Knowing at first hand the horror of war Tegan developed a process of settling disputes that put bloody battle at the end of a list of better options. As a wounded warrior Tegan developed the intellect of the wise woman. Through pain and suffering and constant striving she became a druid to her people. Her battles changed from the earthly plane to the plane of spirit and powerful magic. Even when Tegan became old and weak in her body her very presence among her people was enough to deter the most foolish of attackers or invaders. In time, her people raised a large pile of stones, larger than all the territorial markers around the clan hearth, to hold her presence among her people long after her spirit had passed to the Otherworld.

'Wisdom sits in places.'

On Further Reflection

We become what life, with all its opportunities and threats, makes us. We respond to opportunity by pushing ourselves to achieve what may seem to be a little out of reach or by working outside our comfort zone. We respond to threats by becoming more warlike or more diplomatic.

The choice is up to us, but those around can have a major influence in pushing us forward or deterring us from taking risks. I am never sure what the determining factor is in any particular situation. Perhaps I am not wise enough yet and have more work to do.

Should I tell or write more stories? What do you think?

17

FIONN: A FORCE OF NATURE

Fionn spent his final days in the Shelly Place where he ended
his life in Sligo bay. He opened his veins and gave his
blood to the sea. Most of the stories about Fionn as an old man
are set, appropriately, in the north west, the dying place. This
is where the old sun goes down, going to Hy Brassil where its
life is renewed, making way for a young rising sun the next
morning.

Another story of Fionn has him sitting on Benbulben, on his seat that is so pronounced on the mountain. His boots are off and his feet are in Sligo bay to cool them off in preparation for sunset and final cooling in the ocean. Bran and Sceolán were in the heather at his feet. You can see them there even today: Bran lying down and facing east, checking to see who is coming over the hills above Glen of Aodh, and Sceolán standing up and facing west, checking the way forward.

Fionn hears a loud commotion behind him: shouting, roaring, screeching and all the sounds of a tumult heading his direction. It chilled him and the two dogs turned and faced north and growled. Fionn immediately got hot and bothered. This disruption was preventing him getting ready for bed. He was ready to go down but not before he found what was coming on the north wind. The timing did not suit him yet he had to deal with cold-hearted scoundrels coming to damage Sligo, its creatures and landscape.

Fionn turns his hot and angry face to the north and sees a giant of a man, tall, dark and in a flurry, coming towards him, scattering all the Mother's children to the left and right. Some were being crushed and bruised, some had broken limbs and, worse still, many were dead. Fionn's anger blazed even brighter to see this devastation. He would stop this at once. He reached to his right and grabbed an outcrop of ground – trees, hills and valleys and all – and hauled it up by the roots. He hefted it in his hand. It weighted just right. Fionn swung this mass of warm earth and let it fly towards the encroaching disaster. He was not too accurate and the missile flew a little off target. However, it did what Fionn had intended: it brought the northern invader to a screeching halt and beating a hasty retreat into the cold fastness of the ice caps. The West overcame the North once again.

Fionn felt a little better when he saw it go. The Shelly Place was safe for another while. He could get ready for bed now in the comforting knowledge that he had done his job well. The results of his work are still with us.

Sligo is still beautiful in the pale evening light of the setting sun. Where Fionn pulled the enormous sod from the ground slowly filled with water, fish, birds and that attracted many people to its shores. The Ulster people called it Lough Neagh and made it the centre of their province.

Where the large sod landed, half way between the two major Celtic Isles, it formed an island. It sat so well in the salty water that Mannanáin, the great chieftain of the warm sea, made it his home. His children multiplied around its shores and in the woods that grew on it. The Isle of Man, named for Mannanáin, still sits there.

Fionn spent nearly half his life, the second half, in the west of Ireland. He had sought Saba there after she was taken by the Dark Force of the north to his home in the ice fields. He never did find her. She disappeared. He hoped that she had shape-changed again into a doe and out-ran her captor.

What Fionn did find was a pleasure that lasted for a long time. Saba had been carrying Fionn's child in her womb when the Dark Force took her. Somehow she had managed to evade her captor for long enough to bring her baby into the world and leave it in the safe hands of the does and stags of Benbulben where Fionn found him. Fionn gave his son the name Oisín, 'son of the doe', and took him back to Almu, the home he and Saba had enjoyed for so long. Oisín grew to be a great man in his own right and a strong member of the Fianna that guarded Ireland from all invaders and dark forces. Once again, the old sun gave another life to the young sun.

On Further Reflection

Fionn transposes to Finn for those not comfortable with the Irish language. Fionn, Lugh, Daghda and Diarmait are all transpositions of the Sun, the male force in rural creation. Our ancestors explained the creation of the world in the terms available to them. Their science was the science of nature, the original philosophy of life. Maybe we should pay more attention to what they had to say.

18

THE WAIL OF THE BANSHEE

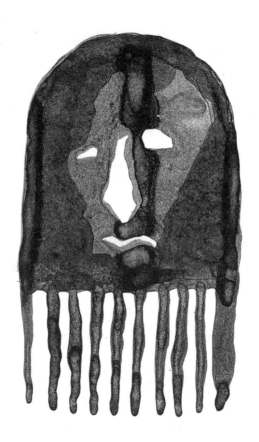

It was December when nights were very long and cold. Darkness set in before we sat down to eat our evening meal and talk about the affairs of the day. A lot of our talk was about times gone by, times when oil lamps were common and radios were rare. Our new radio was already beginning to curb our dinner table discussion. Dan Dare, Pilot of the Future, was on at seven o'clock and my Dad and I were very keen to hear what was happening to him, Joslyn and Digby. Even those names shifted time and space bringing us to Mars, Venus and Jupiter, unknown places of great wonder and adventure. That was much more interesting territory than oil lamps, sods of turf and, God forbid, stories about ghosts.

Bedtime was at nine o'clock. I was about eight years old. The bedroom was warm and cosy. I snuggled under the bed-clothes and cuddled up. That night, as happened sometimes, it was time to hear another short story before sleep invaded my consciousness. My big sister Máire told me a story that left me wondering and a little anxious about how the world worked and changed. I do not remember what story but Máire usually told me about the myths and legends of the local landscape or else about some great adventure we would go on together when we would be older. What ever story she told me that night it left me feeling uncomfortable. It must have been a ghostie.

The bed clothes became much too light and impossible to wrap closely enough around my small shivering form. I rolled them and me into a tight ball without even my nose out and settled down as sleep began to creep into the clothes ball. I was at ease again.

Then it began. What started as a squeal from a cat changed into the long wail of some forlorn and desolate otherworld creature. The wail rose from a low and slow howl to a scream of anguish that chilled my bones. It rose and fell in volume and in tone. The volume at its height blotted out all other sounds and isolated me from the rest of the universe. I felt alone in my

157

ball of clothes and isolated in my awestruck and frightened mind. All other thought and reason was gone. I was in another time and space, in a world of fear and terror. I had been transported by the all-powerful animal wail.

The tone was sharp to begin with but, somehow, became more harsh and hurtful to my ears and psyche. It seared my nervous system and withered my sense of self. I was diminished by a sense of immobilisation, invasion and colonisation. My spirit, self and identity were all touched and marked. It seemed to go on forever in a timeless and eerie void. Even today, after more that half a century, it still chills and haunts me.

The world returned somewhat to normal when I heard my mother's voice calling to me. I stopped listening to the unending and unworldly wail and focussed on my mother's soft and comforting voice. She called gently and drew me out from my ball of clothes, nose first. It was as though I came up for air after a long breath under water. The air in my lungs seemed cold and a little uncomfortable. The bedroom was eerily silent and cold.

My mother sat quietly on the side of the bed with her hand extended to touch my head as I surfaced. Her touch was warm and gentle. She and the family had heard the wailing at the back of the house and my mother came to my room to see if I was awake and worried or asleep and oblivious to the wailing. I was glad to see her. A sense of normality returned when I saw her. She made no mention of the wailing which, by then, had stopped. She talked about small and inconsequential things until my eyeballs went back into my head and I became sleepy for the second time. This did not take long as I was usually exhausted by nine o'clock each night having traversed most of the county at high speed during the day, or so it seemed. I slept quietly after that.

Next day the news of what happened the night before came from an overheard conversation between my mother and a neighbour, Mrs Byrne. She and her family had heard the commotion the night before but had also heard the news of the death of a sister of Mrs McDermott, the next neighbour after the Byrnes, who had another Mc in her maiden name – McMorrow. The sister had died the day before away in England, in London, I think. She had been ill for a long time and her end had come at last. This was ordinary news, nothing for me to get too worried about.

What was extraordinary was what I heard next. The McMorrow name was ancient and the 'Banshee' was said to follow the family, or so Mrs Byrne and my mother agreed. The 'Banshee'? What did that mean? Whatever it meant it was spoken about in a hushed voice and with downcast eyes by the two women on our doorstep. Their folded arms wrapped a little tighter under their breasts as they spoke intently about the events of the day and night before. The whole neighbourhood was full of the talk of it. What Mrs Byrne had to say was what made all jaws fall open. It would remain a story for a long time.

Paddy McDermot came home from work late the evening before and had his food about half past eight. He had just finished his final cup of tea when the wailing began. He and his wife Mollie listened for a while until he finally resolved to put a stop to it. He went out to the yard at the back of the house and picked up two sods of turf as he passed the winter fuel pile. He would shift those cats and give some peace to the neighbourhood before he would put his feet up at the fire. Cats? Apparently not!

He went around the side of the house to the long garden where the wailing was coming from. He was stopped dead in his tracks by what he saw. A small and round-figured old woman, all dressed in a luminous white, long dress was standing behind the garden hedge and apparently combing her hair. She paid no attention to Mr McDermott and continued her wailing. The ground shook under his feet. He was stunned to silence and inaction.

The two sods of turf were still gripped tightly in his fists when he went back into the house. He was a white as a sheet, or so Mrs McDermott had told Mrs Byrne. The sods went into the fire instead of flying through the air but they did not warm Paddy McDermott that night. He felt cold in his soul. Mollie knew immediately what she had already suspected, no, what she expected to be the case. The Banshee came as a herald of the news that would follow the next day. Eileen McMorrow, Mollie's sister, was dead.

Another woman, Mrs Quinn, died a few weeks later. Her maiden name was O'Hara, another very old Sligo name. She lived all her married life near my family home. I was in school with her son, Sean. He was a quiet lad, never in any trouble of any kind and middle of the road in his primary school class. Sean's mother had been ill for as long as I knew him. He hurried home from school each day while we rambled in and out of every nook and cranny of our local environment. Sean had to be available to do messages for his mother or any other work he could do at home. Although her death had been expected for a long time, all were shocked when she finally did pass on. She closed her eyes for the last time at about nine o'clock one evening a few weeks after Eileen McMorrow died.

Again, I was in bed and dozing. The howling started and progressed as before but this time I knew that it was coming from another world and not from our backyard. It lasted for an eternity and my mother appeared again at the time when she was needed most. Again, she put my mind at ease with her easy smile and warm hands as she tucked me in. I slept comfortably holding on to her smile.

As I retell the stories of the Banshee I cannot be sure of any of the remembered details. They seem vague to me and, to a large degree, not relevant. What does remain clear is the awful sound of wailing that seemed to come from the yard at the back of our home. This shrill voice from the other world still rings in my ears whenever I take the time to listen to it and that's not very often. Although I have not heard that sound since I guess it will always be there.

By the way, my mother's maiden name begins with a Mc.

On Further Reflection

This is a true story. I can still feel that cold shudder going through my body over fifty years later. Other people have told me their story of the Banshee, *bean sí*, the Fairy woman. All had their own interpretation of these things but nobody knows what is going on. The stories remain a mystery even in modern times. One friend saw the Banshee in the company of her husband who died a few days later. He could not see the Banshee but she and her son could. Have you seen the Banshee or the Mada Dúbh, the Black Dog, or have you heard them howl? I have.

19

THE DEFEAT OF BALOR
AND THE FOMORIANS

The natural enemies of the Great Mother were the Gods of Winter who came every year to bring devastation to her family. These Lords of Darkness, the Fomorians, came originally from the cold and dark underworld of the north-sea floor, from Faoi Mara. They looked with a blank cold stare of envy at the green valleys and tall trees along the seashore. The Giants of the Ice Lands stood waiting for the signal to go to war. They milled around, well hidden and blanched with fear and yet driven by jealousy and cold anger, in wait for the day when they would reclaim the lands taken from them by their old enemy, Bilé, Lord of Light and Sun and Sky.

Balor, leader of the dreaded Fomorians, lived in their advance outpost in a crystal palace on his island home of Tory, Túr Connaill, off the far north-west coast. He led an advance party to reconnoitre the land of the north-west of Ireland with his evil eye. This eye was huge and callous and in the middle of his forehead. This third eye contained all the withering power of frost, snow and the icy wind from the north. It took one hundred strong warriors to lift its lid in preparation for the seasonal battle. It had to be used on a selective basis as its over use exhausted Balor and then could not be used again for a long time, another year.

It was Balor's grandson, Lugh, the Lord of Light, brother of Brigit, the bright Moon Goddess, who was the only one with enough power to quench the venom and cold spite of the fierce wintry eye of Balor. Even so, Lugh could not melt the cold heart of Balor. Lugh had come out of the darkness and into the light. He abandoned the dark north and moved south on his journey around the world. In Ireland, he found a place to lay his head at night and a place to rise early in peace and quiet that lay undisturbed for millennia.

Lugh had heard rumours and rumblings that Balor was on the move. The land had darkened considerably and Brigit could only bring poor crops for many years recently. The creatures of the land and many fish had moved further south to find enough heat and light to survive. Retreat was the best response to such a formidable foe.

But now it was time to make a stand. It was necessary to send Balor back home before he would bring back the great *cúinneas*, when no living creature could live on land or in the sea. Both sides lined up for war. Balor and Lugh stood back from the battle until it was proven necessary for them to take action. If either were injured their warriors would break ranks and bid a hasty retreat. Each felt it necessary to avoid this at all costs. And the cost was high. Their battle occurred in the war to end all wars when the Lords of Darkness invaded the Shelly Place in the depths of a long harsh winter. Balor captured all the lands north of Uisneach and was pressing for more. The battle swung to and fro between the Lords of Light and the Lords of Darkness.

It was the Well of Healing that enabled the De Danaans, fighting on the side of light and love, to hold out for so long against the incessant onslaught of the cold-hearted Fomorians. When the De Danaan warriors were injured in battle, scorched or broken by the shafts coming from the North, they were dipped in the Well of Healing at Heapstown, just over the hill from the site of the battle. The Formorians knew that this would lose the battle for them if it was not stopped.

A cohort was sent to stop this recovery project, a cohort led by Oct Trialleacht. He gathered the bones of the dead warriors of his own people, the Fomorians and heaped them over the Well sealing it from the De Danaan warriors. As a result, the battle began to swing in favour of the Formorians.

The Ice Lords had taken most of the northern territories and were surging towards the Centre of Power. The Mother was in great danger. Just when it seemed that all was lost, Lugh, the Lord of Light, rose with his warriors in the east and struck a mighty blow. They sent many shafts flying into the battle zone and this stopped the Fomorian onslaught.

165

Some say it was with Lugh's magical spear, a beam of light, a magical weapon of great antiquity, that did the real damage. Others say that it was his simple slingshot, casting a ball of light that delivered the final blow. In either case, the result was the same. Balor had rallied his troops, getting ready for a last and deadly push to overthrow the De Danaans, the people of the eastern sun world. Lugh hurled his weapon of light at Balor who had turned to lead his troops having eyed up the De Danaan warriors, measuring them up for murder.

The power and accuracy of Lugh's throw was so great that it hit Balor straight into his third eye. It tore the head from the shoulders of Balor and shot it into the air. The head spun into the sky like a dark comet before it fell to earth again. It rolled down the hill behind where Balor had made his final rallying call opposite to where Lugh had positioned his risen army. Even in death the eye still had great residual energy. As the head rolled to rest on the valley floor the eye opened for the last time. The searing glare burned a mighty hole in the ground and scorched the hills around it. The battle was over. With Balor dead his Fomorian warriors softened their approach and soon began to slide back into the northern sea sinking in defeat.

'Ni bheid a leithead aris ann!'
[We will never see the likes of them again!]

In time, this scorched hole filled with rainwater, the tears of the many Fomorians who in defeat and anguish retreated north to their frozen wastelands and crystal halls under the cold Dark Sea. It made a fine lake. Today, this lake is called Lough Na Suil, the Lake of the Eye, just a stone's throw from the carn that covers the Well of Healing. It is one of our best trout fishing lakes in the north west, but it has no salmon.

As you wander its shore, rod in hand, you can contemplate the day when the Formorians will invade this countryside again, to reclaim their long lost lands. And invade they surely will. They stand in wait for their time to come. Like the Black Worm and the Black Boar, they are an ongoing threat to us in our everyday lives. Constant vigilance and the protection of the Great Mother and her son, Lugh of the Long Arm, give us the hope of victory.

On Further Reflection

This story tells us about the encroachment of the ice-fields onto the land of Ireland during the last glacial period, which ended 10,000 to 15,000 years ago. It does so in the terms in which it was understood by the earliest people who came to live here shortly after that period, when the ice-sheet was retreating. They spoke in non-technical language as the technology of glacial events was not available at that time. The modern language of eco-systems, tectonic plates and meteorology is just that – modern language. People can only use the concepts and terms available to them. Any problem in understanding what they told us in this story is with our 'modern, scientific' vocabulary.

Balor is the dark eye of winter that sits in the sky opposite the sun. It is co-incident with the moon at full moon. The Fomorians came from the North Sea. Being icebergs they lived and came from under the sea. They destroyed all that grew and froze the land making growth impossible. Water turned to ice, liquids became solid and the air became un-breathable.

Tory as an out-post, a crystal palace on his island home of Tory, Túr Connáill, was the home of the *tóraíoch*, the renegade people on the run. The crystal palace was made of ice of course. Conall was the first leader of the Ui Connáill clan, the O'Donnell's of Donegal, Tir Connáill, the country of Connáill.

Lugh is the sun that drove Balor from the land. He rose in the east and fought with shafts of light and balls of heat to melt the hearts and resolve of the Fomorians and to push them off-shore. The Túatha Dé Danaan, the people of Danú, came in from the east where the sun rises. Danu, as spoken of in the Danube River, was roughly co-incident with the lower limit of the ice-fields in central Europe. It was the ice-fields that drove many people out of northern Europe and into Ireland 15,000 years or so ago. They came with the sun and lived at the edge of the melting ice.

Injured or damaged leaders had to be rejected because their injury indicated that they were not favoured by the Mother. If not favoured, their people would not flourish and may not even survive.

The Well of Healing takes a little thinking about. Water quenched thirst and fire when the sun was too hot. Ice was made better by melting back to the water state. Pure water from the body of the Mother cleansed the body of toxins or poisons. This detoxing is a major element of all medications even today, but was even more so in earlier times.

The placebo effect of imbibing 'pure' water or 'purified' chemical mixtures is very powerful in healing. Covering the Well of Healing at Heapstown with the bones of dead Fomorian warriors, or stones, meant that the hardened spirits of the stones overcame the softer spirits of pure water. War and cold-hearted conquest temporarily overcame wisdom and negotiation.

Maigh Tuireadh was the Plain of Towers, the plain filled with boulders dropped by the ice-sheet when it retreated. The Cailleach, with her apron full of 'erratic' stones, was at work again.

20

A Tour of the Sligo Landscape

They were a small group. The women in the group seemed happier, more relaxed, and they chatted easily while they waited for me to begin. The men, on the other hand, shuffled their feet, seemed a bit distracted and even a little impatient. One couple came from Texas and seemed to be a bit 'new age'. The German couple were reserved and polite, and had enquired earlier about the anthropology of the people who had lived at Carrowmore. They didn't seem to realise that the site had such a long history and that so many people had been there from so many parts of the old world. The three Japanese women were talking continuously and were very excited at the prospect of a guided tour. It was time to begin.

'Is mise Micheál agus beidh mise agaibh ar an turas.'

The women laughed while the men looked a bit bewildered. I grinned at my little bit of mischief and felt assured that I now had their attention.

'My name is Michael and as we go on our tour please feel comfortable to ask any question you may have. If you see anything that reminds you of what you have seen on your travels around the world, please comment so that we can develop a discussion on what is here at Carrowmore. This will ensure that your areas of interest are addressed and that you enjoy your tour to the full.'

There was a general hubbub of conversation and nods of understanding about my comments.

'Today you are in Ireland, in Sligo, in the northwest. Sligo gets its name from the Irish word *sligeach*, which means 'the place of shells'. Even today the coastline is rich in cockle, mussel and winkle. The oyster beds were over fished in the 1900s but small quantities are still available along the south coast at Culeera.

Some say that the original name was Slí an Eac, the 'way of the horse', as the ford of the river in Sligo is the main route through to Dún na Gall, Donegal, the Fort of the Strangers, but I have no story about this. For me, Sligo is the Shelly Place.

The earliest inhabitants of the Shelly Place came soon after the end of the last ice age. They came from the sea and settled where Sligo town is today. They hunted and gathered all over the Culeera peninsula, to the west of where they lived. Coill Iorra, the Wood of the Squirrels, is now grassland with no habitat for squirrels. The trees were cleared many centuries ago.

The men roamed the mountains in search of larger game. Red deer were plentiful and boar hunted for truffles in the woods. Hare and bear added excitement to the hunt and food to the table. They cleared an oval nematon at the highest point of Culeera. By ringing the trees inside this area, taking a strip of bark away all the way around the trunk, they defoliated the trees and allowed sunshine to reach the ground. This allowed grass and fresh vegetation to grow among the bare trees. Animals used this fresh vegetation for food and drank from the small turlough lake in the back field. Hunters waited to take advantage of this easy supply of meat. It was less necessary to travel to hunt by arranging the nematon at Culeera. In time the trees fell down. This site became associated with the bounty of the Great Earth Mother and was, in time, considered sacred and a site of rite-of-passage rituals.

The earliest people fished the seas on all three sides of the peninsula and gathered seaweed and shelled creatures for food. Mainly the women gathered what was available from the nearby woodlands and waterways and supplied eighty to ninety per cent of the food supply. The kitchen middens found along the shores show ample evidence of shell fishing for seasonal food: cockle, mussel, winkle and oyster.

Men hunted for larger game in the outlying areas. This relieved pressure on the local food supply, but meat did not store well at that time. The permafrost was retreating and the warm, sub-tropical climate made meat turn putrid in a short space of time. This made meat a rare treat enhancing its symbolic value. This higher status food also supplied bone and antler/horn for tool making as well as skins for clothing people and coverings for hearth and homes.

The early people camped along the south shore at Culleen-amore and Culleenduff, dumped the empty shells close to where they fished and brought the meat back home. Where the shell dumps or middens accumulated there is more than three thousand meters of middens. Many were destroyed by the rising sea levels. One that remains contains about 25,000 tonnes of shells.

Evidence of their campsites still exists. These sites, on top of the middens, were of a temporary nature used only during fishing seasons. The shell food was not a mainstay of their diet but, as an additive, did give an essential mineral and vitamin balance so necessary to the good health of those early people. These hunting and gathering people lived well from the fruit of the land. A comfortable living was there for the taking for the people of the place of shells and they lived long and well.

The peninsula of the Wood of the Squirrel is about eight kilometres long and five kilometres at its widest point. The red squirrel was plentiful and thrived on rich pickings. It was said that a squirrel could climb a tree on Malin Head in north

Donegal and travel south to Mizen head in Cork without touching the ground. Culeera and the entire island were heavily forested in the Stone Age, mainly with large elm trees, and had a sub-tropical climate. This warm climate gave food for the wild creatures for nearly eleven months of the year.

When these elms, giants of the woods, were ringed they lost their foliage and their lives. This clearing of the forest caused some major changes to the landscape. Grasses grew where the sun revitalised the earth and lakes accumulated in the valleys, made from the waters not siphoned away by the dead trees. A Mediterranean-style weather pattern gave year-round grazing for deer and other indigenous animals. Coppicing and pollarding trees gave extra food for the animals and for people. Animals such as deer liked to live at the edge of the forest using it as safe cover, but also spent some time in the sunlit *ur lars*, the green floors, where the trees had been cleared. This is why the nematon was cleared by the early people. If so, they also found it a good place to meet and celebrate life and all its changes. Life was good and the communities thrived.'

'What kind of society did they have?' It was one of the Texans speaking.

'Women were central to the social order,' I replied. 'The bearing and rearing of children was the most pressing issue in their community whose sustenance depended on the fecundity of its womenfolk. The hunters ensured that food was readily available but, as the population density grew, they also performed the task of protectors of the community from attacks from wild animals and any rogue element in the society at large. At Carrowmore the age profile of the people whose remains have been recovered and tested for Carbon 14 content has been surprising. The youngest was a pre-natal baby in late

174

pregnancy. This baby was buried beside its mother in one of the large boulder circles. Males and females in all the decades were found up to sixty years of age. One archaeological dig uncovered the remains of a man of sixty years or more, a great age and well beyond what was expected for people of that time. Some of the structures contained as many as fifty people while others contained only two or three. In total, only 200 have been found to date out of an estimated population of 500,000 but more on that later.

People lived in family groups. They congregated along the banks of the Garavogue River that flows through Sligo and close to the mouth of the estuary. At that time, in the period of change between nomadic hunting and gathering and settled farming, they went home to their thatched houses each evenings unless they were on an extended hunt. This is where they lived, became mothers and fathers, and watched their children as they grew up, strong and healthy. The men hunted and the women bore children from puberty to menopause. After that they stayed home to take care of children allowing the stronger and more youthful ones to do the work. If any was injured and could not work they often became the shamans and medicine people of their clan. They passed their memories on to their grandchildren who became the gifted ones of later generations.

They celebrated all the important passage points of the year and in life, marking the turning of the wheels of the world and the coming and going to and from this world. Rites of passage at birth, puberty, marriage, at the end of their productive years and finally, at death were given prime time. The selection and inauguration of a new chieftain or the recognition of a new craft worker was celebrated. The fire festivals of Imbolc, Beltine, Samhain and Lughnasa marked the four corners of the year and other celebrations were organised around these dates.'

'How did they celebrate these events?' asked the Japanese girl who had seemed the most shy and then lit up the place with a big smile.

'A large oval was cleared in the Elm forest and used as a sacred space. It was made more sacred by years of celebration and ritual performed there. Such sites, originally nemetons for hunting, have been found all over Europe. The fallen trees rotted away leaving green fields for crops and animals. What has been found here, at Carrowmore, is a set of stone structures laid out in an oval clearing but in a spiral pattern. This spiral leads from the entrance portals and finishes at Listoghal, site 51, as Petrie numbered it. Tomb 51 is at a focal point in the oval clearing and in the regional landscape. Ceremony and ritual were practised here for more than 5,000 years, from earliest dates of 5,400 BC to the latest, 90 AD. No habitation sites or waste material has been found here suggesting that people did not live here and the site was for ceremony only. Later, the sites of particular festivities were marked with stone structures.

'OK, Mike,' said the man from Texas. 'But where did they come from? Were they Celts?'

'The people who were here came over a long period of time. If they built their earliest structures 7,400 years ago, as the recent archaeological evidence suggests, it's likely that they arrived here 8,000 to 9,000 years ago. This was a long time ago, 5,000 years before the Celts. The earliest people were small, dark-skinned, dark-haired, dark-eyed and slightly stooped. They may have come directly from North Africa, through Iberia and by sea along its western coasts following the Atlantic currents. This is the most likely route. Later, more came through the three major routes through Europe. Old stories tell of people coming from the cities of the plains of India but this is unlikely. The Indo-European people would have come from East Africa originally, travelled up the Nile and settled in the Fertile Crescent. They gathered in Asia Minor and spent a long time there, where Turkey and Greece are today. Here they learned to be Europeans.

Then some went north, to the Ukraine, and then through the north of Europe, through Germany, Denmark, on to Scandinavia and by sea to Scotland and from there through the Black Door of the North. It is known as the Black Door because the sun never shines from that point in the sky. These people were called the Scythe or Scythiens, the Scoti or proto-Celtic people. They populated the Antrim coast and, in time, moved south through the island.

Some came through the great Inland Sea, the Mediterranean, sailing to Malta, Italy and along the eastern coasts to the Iberian Peninsula. From here they sailed up the Ebo River, carried their boats over the mountains to the sea at Santander. From there they followed the run of the great western ocean, sailing into the mouth of the setting sun. They passed the southern coast of Cornwall, rounding the southern tip of Ireland to make landfall either on the White Door of the south where the sun was always in residence or through the Red Door of the setting sun on the west coast.

The third highway through Europe was along the route of the Danube River, the longest river in Europe. This river got its name from the ancient Earth Mother, Danu or Anu, and it led our people through Austria and Germany to the Rhine River and on through Belgium and Holland to the western sea. From here the coast of England was an easy voyage away and Wales was an easy trail to the western coast. From Wales they came through the Grey Door of dawn, on the east coast of Ireland, to the island at the edge of the known world.

The Boyne river estuary gave easy entry and access to the rich lands of the fertile river valley. These were the Celtic people. Their name derived from the decorative art work done on bone, horn and stone. Here they built their biggest and best structures. Then with weakened spirit and diminished intent they moved westwards to Carrowmore. This route led them through Loughcrew (Sliabh na gCailleach) to Sí Beag and Sí Mór in South Leitrim, over the rugged karst mountains at Carrowkeel, Ceathru Caol, the narrow quarter, and on to Culeera where they created Carrowmore. That was the history we had until ten years ago. It was thought that the Boyne Valley was where the Passage Tomb tradition began.

Today, thanks to the archaeologists, we know better. The early people came to Carrowmore first and then developed their tradition as they moved eastwards towards the Boyne Valley. Carrowmore's earliest date is nearly 1,500 years older than the earliest dates at Bru na Boinne, the hostel in the Boyne Valley. To give all this perspective I should tell you that the Bru is about 1,500 years older than the current dates associated with the pyramids of Egypt and Stonehenge in the south of England. There may be some more interesting relations between the sites, but we'll hear more of that later. But, in fairness, the old stories did tell us that our people came in ships from the sky on the west coast. It must have been very cloudy that day. Maybe there is some truth in these old stories after all!'

Miko was the best speaker of English among the Japanese trio. 'So, what did they build and why?' she asked.

'In Carrowmore three basic structures were built in the nemeton that was already cleared and in use for a long period of time. First, let's consider the simplest and probably the oldest design. A ring of large stones, usually thirty-two, each stone between one to two meters in diameter, and each ring between ten and thirty meters in diameter. Such a ring is called a *team-pall* in Irish. This sounds like the word 'temple' used in many languages today. The word *templum* in Latin derives from the same root. It must be said at this point that Irish is the oldest spoken language in Europe and is a remnant of a much older language that was spoken throughout Europe up to the rise of the Roman Empire.

The second type of structure is the Dolmen-like structure, a group of upright stones, three to seven in number and between one and three meters in height. A capstone was hauled on top of these. The capstone is usually the largest of the stones. Dolmen means 'stone table' in the Breton language. The upright stones, usually granite, lean inwards against each other. The capstone is usually made from a rounded boulder that has had half its bulk shattered off in a fire or flattened by hammering. This flattened face sits on top of the uprights and locks the structure in place. The finished shape was quite phallic in form although some say that it looks more skull-shaped.

The third type of structure is really a combination of the first two, a dolmen in the middle of a stone circle. The classic passage tomb design seemed to develop from this third structure. At first a pathway was built, about one meter wide, between the dolmen and the inner edge of the stone circle, joining a pathway that circled the inside of the boulder ring. This radial path was later lined with tall stones, tall enough to allow a slab roof to go over it. At this stage of development it would have looked like a court tomb as much as a passage tomb. The corbelled design of the central chamber developed later and is first seen at Carrowkeel in southeast Sligo, thirty kilometres southeast and 500 to 700 years later than Carrowmore. This is a development of the dolmen structure and also, incidentally, of the first stage of the development of the flying buttress which featured strongly in sacred buildings at a much later time.'

'Can you suggest why circles and standing stones'? Gerhard spoke up from the side of the group. 'Why not squares, triangles or rectangles? Was there some reason for picking these curved shapes?'

'Well, that's a tough one. What I'm about to tell you is not popular with some people who don't accept this proposal, but in the absence of anything better here goes. I hope that you will give it a hearing. The circle, the opening, is the eternal symbol of the woman who was central to very early society. As the bearer of children she was essential to the continuity of the group. Without successful birthing and rearing of children extinction came quickly.

The male had the role of protector and provider of food, and was symbolised by the erect stones, a phallic structure. These structures existed separately and combined. Placing the dolmen inside the circle has an obvious suggestion embedded, symbolic of the procreation process.

In the combined form, at first, a path was built from the upright centre close to but not quite to the inner edge of the timpeall of stones. Later, this path was roofed to form a closed passage. This passage was the symbol of the compromise made by the protected women and the protecting men to ensure a stable society.

In the Boyne Valley, at the other end of the tradition, these structures were covered with stones. This seems to have happened some time after the initial construction of the combination structures. This is suggested by the fact that many of the stones in the stone circle are marked on their inner face as well as their outer face but are now covered by the carn.

An interesting story about Dún Aengus, the central site in the Boyne Valley, relates to what happens there each year at the winter solstice. When all is dormant or dead in the body of the Earth Mother and the ravages of the Dark Lords of Winter threaten to annihilate all of creation, a miracle occurs. The wild creatures have gone away or into hibernation. The sun is low in the sky and the world is a threatened and cold place and appears as dying.

Then, at sunrise, on the morning of the solstice, a male Sun God, the Daghda Mór, rises and sends a shaft of light into the passage of the mound at Newgrange, into the body of the Mother. The passage, the entrance to the body of the Mother, is twenty metres long and leads through to the internal chambers. The side chambers are her ovaries. The central and back chamber forms her womb. By this ritual process, the mother is fertilised and new life begins.

The next day, the sun begins to return again to the sky, the temperature begins to rise and the flora and fauna begin a new cycle of growth. Spring has sprung. A rebirth occurs. In this way the ancients co-operated with their God in the creation of the universe. If you want a name for the Earth Mother in those very early times, then I would suggest the name Brí or Brigid. Her name has the same root as the word 'bright'. This name associates her particularly with the moon. This also would also tie her to Knock na Rae that translates from *Cnoc na Rea* as the Hill of the Moon. The moon was also associated with hunting and, in fact, the October Moon is called the Hunter Moon. Maebh was strongly associated with hunting and warfare.

Carrowmore does not have the classical form of a passage tomb as found in the Boyne Valley, but does have all the elements that went to make a classic passage tomb. With that said, Site 27 is a fine stone circle with a well defined, central cruciform centrepiece, the oldest in Ireland. Here our earliest people conceived the idea of co-operating with their God in the work of creation and built these simple but ingenious structures for the perennial celebration of the mystery of life.

When you stand at Site 51 you can see the two great carns on the extremes of the landscape. Here at 51 is another, smaller carn. The local stories call it the Giant's Grave. As in most Irish stories, the giant is Fionn mac Cumhal, leader of the Fianna. Fionn's task was to defend the country from internal threats and invasions from the sky, the sea and from under the ground. Fionn as a young man lived in the east coast of Ireland. His summer camp was at the Hill of Allen in County Kildare and all his earlier adventures – fighting spectres, giants and strange people – took place in that part of Ireland. As an older and less valiant man he came west to the Shelly Place and many of the stories of him in the latter part of his life occur here. The epic story of Diarmait and Gráinne culminates in the mountains north of Sligo city. The insight that it gives into the value system of our early people could not be done justice as an aside to this story. It has to be a story for another day. Fionn, of course, was the Bronze Age version of the sun god that rose in the eastern world, crossed the sky and set in the west. As he set and sank into the ocean he gave his life's blood to the sky and the sea, and that's why, even today, we have red sunsets and the Red Door of the west.

But real people lived and died here. Although over 200 remains of people have been found at Carrowmore so far, this is a small number considering the fact that somewhere between 500,000 and 750,000 people would have lived in this area during the period of use as a sacred site. About fifty cremated remains were found in Tomb 4, one of the smallest and the tomb with the oldest associated dates. The largest tomb and the most recent, Site 51, contained the remains of only five adults and two children. In this case they were inhumed, not cremated. Most of the other sites where remains were found had only one or two remains in place. The conclusion that I draw from this is that burials were secondary to the purpose of these sites. In 1,000 years' time, if the remnants of today's cathedrals were excavated, some human remains would be found. This would not make the structures any the less cathedrals and would not, certainly, make them cemeteries.

The focal location of Site 51 gives rise to another, more recent myth, a modern one but nonetheless interesting. If you draw a line across the globe from Carrowmore, through the Boyne Valley, and continue it across Europe, it passes through the cities of Paris and Rome and continues to the site of the pyramids at Giza. At Carrowmore we have the three structures, offset by twenty degrees from a straight line. The watercourse formed by the lake at Lough Gill, the Garavogue River and the estuary runs to the north of the alignment. In the Boyne Valley, three structures – Knowth the place of Light; Dowth, the place of Darkness; and Newgrange, or Dun Aengus to give it its older name – have the Boyne River flowing to the south. At Giza, the three pyramids form the same pattern and have the Nile River flowing to the east. High in the sky we have the original of the pattern. Orion, the great constellation of the ancients, has three bright stars in its belt and the Milky Way lies to its side. This constellation has a great deal of mythology associated with it but, again, that's a story for another time. Whether there is a connection between Carrowmore and Giza or not is still up for discussion, but the coincidences are certainly entertaining. But, for now, back to Carrowmore.'

'Where did all these stones come from?' asked Miko. 'How did they get to where they were used?'

'The granite stones came from the Ox Mountains to the south and east. They were carried here by the flow of ice at the end of the last ice age about 10,000 to 12,000 years ago. It was made originally when the two continental plates of the Atlantic floor and Europe crashed into each other 600 million years ago. The magma welled up and solidified to make the mountain range. The limestone came from the old sea bed. It was laid down by a great river that flowed out of Europe maybe 320 million years ago. It was crushed up and pushed to the sea by the ice sheets also.

I do like the old story, that the Cailleach was carrying stones in her apron to make the Carn for Mebh, or was it Brí, and her apron split as she passed over Carrowmore. I like the coincidence between the ice sheet and her apron. The Cailleach was the tough side of the Great Mother.

The items manufactured by these people, and found on these sites show, in miniature and in full size, a selection of their tools and other items of ornament. These include axe-heads, hammerheads, arrowheads, cutters, scrapers, needles and beads. These seem to have been for bodily decorations but also may have been symbols of office for those craft magicians in the tribe. One type of item that has not been well explained is the baetyl, the egg-shaped and spherical stones found along with the remains of people. One possible explanation is found in the Chinese and Native American traditions. This tells that the stone would have been used in the cremation ceremony and would have been a haven for the soul of that person when the body was burned. Later, it would have been worn by a young woman in her pouch on a string around her neck, or if it were a larger baetyl it would be kept near her sleeping place. As the young woman became pregnant and the foetus began to grow, the soul would transfer to the new body and be reborn at full term. This was their way of keeping their gifted people in their community. Perhaps this was also the case with our stone age people.

We don't have an official explanation, one agreed with the archaeologists or anthropologists, of the spiral pattern formed by the cromlechs ('curves of stones') as they swing through the portals of the site set at Tomb 7 and Tomb 13 and continue in a beautiful curve to Tomb 51. One possible explanation is that the priests and acolytes celebrated at each of the sites, starting at the beginning of the new year and culminating at the high summer festival. The suggestion is that each tomb or site was used to celebrate an aspect of the culture and social system of the early communities. These would have been repeated each year to mark the passage points of time. This pattern may have given the idea for such Christian practises as the Stations of the Cross or the Pattern Masses that were so popular in the Sligo area until recent times. These were Masses held in the homes of the people on a rotation basis in the spring and autumn of each year, to which family, friends and neighbours were invited.

The mountains and hills that surround Culeera on the eastern side form one of its boundaries. The other boundary is formed by the watercourse from Lough Gill along the Garavogue River to the estuary and along the beach from Cumeen strand. Míosagán Maebh (Maebh's Carn), high up on Knock na Rae, marks one end of the landside boundary. Maebh's story is from the time of bronze age/iron age. She was the warrior chief of the western province of Conn. Her husband was Allill who came from Donegal in Ulster. His summerhouse, Grianan an Ailleach, can still be seen high in the hills above the road that goes between Letterkenny and Derry City. This couple lived at Crúachan in County Roscommon. It was from there that they set out on the epic adventure, the Táin Bó Cuailgne, to bring a bull from Ulster to Connaught.

The story is set in the Bronze or Iron Age, 2,000 years ago but the carn of stones was there for more than 3,000 years before that. The original incumbent was known by many different names. The one I like best in this context is Brigid, the huntress, associated with the moon. As such she embodies all the aspects of the Mother Earth, the female aspect of God. Knocknarea or Cnoc Na Rea, in old Irish, translates in a number of ways. Knocknarae is a gibberish word, a kind of phonetic spelling in English phonemes of the old Irish name. It was corrupted by too many spellings by people who either did not know or appreciate the more ancient tongue or, in some cases, had a vested interest in changing the names so that records and legalities became more complex and ancient title would be obscured.

Brigid's or Maebh's male counterpart is located on Carns Hill on the other end of the land boundary, just above the lake. Dagda Mór was the father figure that mated with Maebh but in earlier times Bilé and Brigid played their part in the creation mythic tradition of the Shelly Place. Between them they gave life to all the creatures who lived in this region. This included all the grasses, flowers, trees, insects, animals, fish, birds and, of course, people that inhabited the wood of the squirrels. The names that I've used here are the names used by the people of the later Celtic people and before that the proto-celts. The names used by the earliest people have been obscured or have had new names superimposed on them and have become confused in the memories of our people. *Is brón an scéal é. [It is a sad story.]*

Each species of creature was created by being named and each reflected an aspect of God in their character. God, in fact, contained all the characteristics of creation and the process of creation itself. It was for this reason that the early people selected totem animals to teach them the wisdom of God. In fact, it appears that they had only one God, the early duality or recognition of or separation of God from his people. This may also explain the remains of animals and birds found on the sites at Carrowmore. The bones of small birds such as thrush, blackbird, duck and goose are found in abundance in some of the sites. Shell fish and fish with backbones are also common finds. Bones of small animals such as squirrel, hare, wolf, dog and cat were found buried within the stone circles. Larger animals such as sheep, goat, pig and deer were also common and, at a later stage, the cow and the horse.

The hare, like the salmon, has been a creature associated with wisdom by many of our people. Both appear in the symbols of the city and county of Sligo. The hare goes forward in leaps and bounds of the imagination. The salmon swims in his own environment and leaps into the air to plunge again to the depths of the river, a symbol of the intuitive leap of the imagination so appreciated by people who gained greatly by the creativity of early genius. This could also explain who the people were that were interred at Carrowmore. The people, the gifted ones, the smiths in stone and wood, the hunters and growers of crops, the healers of the body and the mind, the Anam Caras or Soul Friends, and those who taught and developed the wisdom of the ancients, were reincarnated to keep them and their talents in the community.

Tomb 51 is a focal point in the landscape. The sites in the immediate area are oriented towards Tomb 51 in a variety of ways. For example, the stone circles or timpealls have a space where a stone has been pulled to one side, possibly to form an entrance, on the side oriented to site 51. The dolmen structures also have their apparent entrances pointing towards site 51.

There are some nice local stories about Site 51 that may give some insight to its original purpose. When Fionn, leader of the defenders of Ireland, died and sank into the ocean his blood coloured the horizon, the sea and the sky, to create the Red Door of the west. Later, when the local people found his bones washed up on the shore, they brought them to Carrowmore and piled them high where Site 51 is today.

This story takes on an even richer texture when we consider it along with another more universal story. In the earliest time, the Great Father and Great Mother gave birth to two children. One grew up to be a great warrior chief while the other grew to be a shaman or druid. In time, the druid overcame the warrior. The body of the warrior was dismembered, and de-fleshed.

The bones were used to make the mountains and stones. The flesh was used to make the earth and the blood was used to make the watercourses; the lakes, the rivers and the sea. All the warrior's thoughts were used to make the clouds of the sky.

Between Maebh's carn and Dagda's carn, on the landside, there are ranges of mountains and hills, which seem to mark the southern and eastern limits of the Culeera peninsula. On the top of many of these peaks, cairns similar to the ones on the extremes on Knock na Rae and Carns Hill are clear to see and have some interesting names. One, on the Dartry mountains, is called the House of Caillaigh a Vera, or Carn Caillaigh a Bheara, is said to be the home of the Earth Mother in her less palliative mode. The Caillaigh was said to have carried the stones to build Maebh's carn in the sheet of her apron, from the Hill of Keash. Her apron split with the weight of stones and they fell to the ground at Carrowmore. This seems to be how the action of the glacier was explained. The cairn on the top of the Hill of Keash, or the Hill of Torment, is called the Principle. On the back of this hill is a great cave system associated with many of the old stories.

One story tells of how an old woman chased her run-away cow into the cave late one evening. She ran after the cow all

191

night long in the dark, holding the cow's tail. The next morning she and the cow emerged at Cruachain, the site of Maebh's citadel but, of course, long before Maebh's time. This story seems to relate how the Cailleach, the tough side of the Mother, created the underground cave system, made in ancient times by a great underground river. The opening in the ground at Cruachan is known as Uaimh na gCat, the Cave of the Cats. It was from here that came many of the plagues that devastated the province of Con. Hoards of hounds and pigs, with white bodies and red ears, ran rough-shod over the plains of Conn from here. Plagues of bats and other creatures also emerged to torture the countryside.

East and north of Keash is the Dartry range of mountains. The name translates from the Irish as the Hills of the Stags. On top of many of these hills are cairns of the passage tomb type. This continues along this range of hills to Kings Mountain at the Dromahaire, Druim Da hÉthair, Ridge of the Two Demons, end of Lough Gill. They seemed to mark the boundaries of the peninsula of Culeera. A high percentage of these hilltop cairns are also oriented towards Carrowmore.

The watercourse, flowing from the Lough Gill, the lake of the bright-faced girl, Loc Gealla, at one end, to where Maebh overlooks the estuary at the other end formed the northern boundary. The Garavogue River joins the two together. The river of the Garbh Oc, the Woman of Experience and Wisdom, is the river of life flowing from birth to death, joins with the extremes to give the Three Faces the Goddess, the same one who is the Mother of Aengus, the Mac Ind Oc, of the Boyne valley. The name Aengus or Aongus comes from the old Irish *aon gas*, meaning the One Son of the great mother, a universal theme. The lake is the womb chamber, the river is the birth canal and the estuary is the uterus of the Mother. By marking the boundaries in this way the people of our most ancient times were seen to live in the arms of their god. The dual became the triple in the Mother, the Father and the Son. These were symbolised in the triple spiral of the Boyne valley.

At Site 51 some markings that were first found by some visitors in the middle 1990s. They were viewing a slide show at the visitor's centre when a slide of the capstone of Site 51 was shown. When the slide show was finished they enquired about the markings that seemed so clear to them but had remained unnoticed until that day. The marks were showing on the eastern face of the stone. They were forms of circles within circles touching and open on the bottom tangent and with pockmarks in the middle of the smaller circle. They look like the Greek letter Omega. These and variations of them, side by side, filled the face of the stone. At a later time one of the local archaeologists investigated the marks using rice paper rubbings and infrared photography. The continuing research revealed another mark on the top, inner face, of the pointed, upright stone on the eastern side of the central feature at Site 51. This looked like the number three with the centre limb extended and bent to the left, with a dot at the end of it.

These marks, as yet have not been given any official explanation but some interesting proposals have been put forward. The circles suggest the rising and setting sun or moon. Why the symbol should be repeated has not had even an attempted proposal. Another suggestion is that they symbolise the rising and setting of Mercury and Venus, the inner planets that form loops in the sky on a day to day basis. This has some nice co-relations with Roman and Greek myths. Mercury in the Roman tradition equates to Hermes in the Greek tradition. He was a messenger of the Gods and one of his symbols was the cairn of stones.

The three limbed symbol has been compared to the UM symbol of India. This is symbol of the Universal Vibration or Universal Energy. This would fit in nicely with the stories of the early people of India. The other coincidences are remarkable. Ogham was the ancient Irish God of writing and markings on stone. In Irish the G is softened by the h and so the name is pronounced, using English phonemes as Oam, very like the Indian Um. There may be a relationship between this symbol and Ogham, the old god of writing and marking stones. He is in one of the Carns on top of Carns Hill, on the eastern horizon.

Another relevant coincidence is that the ancient Irish myths and legends have much the same story line and character descriptions, suggesting the same social order and territorial layouts as the ancient Indian myths and legends. Just one more thing, the Irish language is one of the remnants, still living, of a language that was spoken throughout Europe until the rise of the Roman Empire. Some of the words in Irish are quite the same, phonetics and meanings, as in the Sanskrit language of India. Other remnants are found throughout many other European languages.

So, between India and Egypt, we have a nice international story developing. That's appropriate in many ways because the people who came here over the millennia came from many parts of the world. They did not come here in a flock, like swallows. They left groups behind as they persisted in pushing on to the edge of the known world. These intrepid explorers were the equivalent to the astronauts of the twentieth century. Many of these characteristics are still to be seen in our people. The fierce independence of mind, tenacity of purpose and a spirituality that comes from our early appreciation of God is still with us. Was it any wonder that Jesus Christ, the hero of a new day, and his teachings, were so readily accepted from the patrician missionaries?

Well, I hope you enjoyed our tour, a tour through the past of our ancestors, as seen through our myths, legends and the rich archaeological and anthropological heritage. Who knows what continuing research will bring to our attention!

Go raibh míle maith agaibh.
[Thank you very much.]

Go mbeire muid beo ag an am seo arís!
[That we may live well until the next time.]

On Further Reflection

It has taken a lifetime to learn some of the story of Sligo, Carrowmore and the place where I live. I don't remember where a lot of this story comes from. Maybe it is in my bones and leaks out or has to be expressed like mothers mild to relieve some tension in me. As a child I often had a pain in my stomach with curiosity and could only relieve that pain by reading or, better still, running like a wild creature through the story-filled landscape where I grew up.

The pain has subsided since but I still feel the urge to tell story, to relate a narrative that explains the world to me and sometimes to other people. I can't help it. It is in the marrow of my bones.

GLOSSARY OF NAMES, PLACES AND TERMS

Aengus or Oenghus, a god of love, was a son of the Daghda, the main male god and Boann, the goddess of the Boyne River. He lived in Brú na Bóinne, Newgrange.

Ailill, husband of Maebh, whose home, the Grand hat, is still on the hill near the road between Letterkenny and Derry City.

Almu is near Naas in County Kildare. It was the childhood home of Fionn MacCumhaill, the leader of the Fianna.

Anam Cara, meaning soul-mate, is a friend who acts as a spiritual guide.

Badhbh, pronounced Bov in English, meaning rage or violence, was the war goddess who took the form of a raven or hooded crow.

Balisodare, one of the many homes or graves of the Cailleach.

Balor of the Evil Eye was the leader of the Fomorians who invaded Ireland. He was an anti-sun god of the north.

Banshee, a gibberish form of *Bean Sí*, the Fairy woman associated with death.

Beal Easa Dara, the Town at the Rapids of the Oak Forest, is a small village in County Sligo called Ballisodare today.

Bean Feassa, a woman of knowledge, a wise woman, usually involved with healing rites.

Bealtine, the fire festival of the month of May, which celebrates fertility and growth.

Ben Bulben, Mountain of the Black Bear (*see* Gulbáin).

Bilé, Lord of the Universe.

Bó Buí, the yellow cow, is one of the four cows of the Cailleach.

Bran and Sceolán, Fionn's magical sons of she-wolf Tuireann.

Breas or Brés was the tyrannical stand-in for the injured Nuada until his arm was replaced by Dian Cecht. Brés's father, Elatha, was Fomorian and his mother, Eri was De Danaan.

Brehon Laws, based on ideas of 'the responsibilities of the steward', a law system used in Ireland before the imposition of English law in the 1800s based on ideas of 'the rights of the king'.

Brigit, derived from Brí, was a sun goddess and daughter of the Daghda.

Brú na Bóinne, the hostel on the Boyne, is a prehistoric heritage site in Co Meath which includes Newgrange.

Cailleach is the veiled older woman. In iconic terms, the winter female force that destroy nature to make way for new growth in spring.

Carn, cairn in Scotland, is a large construction of loose stones.

Carn Caillaigh a'B héara, a carn on the Dartry Mountains above Balisodare.

Carrowmore, meaning the Large Quarter, is west of Sligo town and the largest megalithic burial ground in Ireland.

Cliabh solus is the sword of light or enlightenment.

Cromlechs, small, oval, self-supporting constructions of stones.

Cruachán Ái, in County Roscommon near the village of Tulsk, was the administrative centre for the province of Connaght.

Cu Chulain, the Hound of Chulain, called Setanta originally, was the epitome of the warrior but much of his extensive narrative suggests he was a warrior of the spirit world.

Danu, Dana, Anu or Áine, was the Mother Goddess of the De Danaan people and gave her name to the river Danube.

De Danaans were the people of the river goddess Danu.

Daghda, the good god, of the De Danaans.

Diarmait, or Diarmaid, of the love-spot or dimple, Gráinne's partner.

Dooney, a gibberish form of Dun Aodh, the stronghold of Hugh.

Druim Dhá Eithiar, the Ridge of the Two Water Demons at Dromahair in County Leitrim.

Eamhain Macha, the administrative centre for Ulster.

na Fianna, a band of warriors that defended Ireland against invasions.

Finn mc Cool, a commonly used form of Fionn MacCumhaill, was called Demna at birth, changed to Fionn, meaning blonde, the colour of his hair.

Fionn, see above.

Fionnabhair, meaning Blonde-headed, was a daughter of Maebh.

Fír Bolg druid tree centre at Uisneach's Aill na Muireann, the Rock of Divisions, the place where the Fir Bold five provinces met in County Roscommon.

Formorians, from *faoi mara* meaning 'under the sea', are the people of the far north, the Ice People.

Fraoch, meaning heather, married Fionnabhair.

Garb O'c, meaning 'rough person, the original name for the Garavogue river in Sligo. A milder translation is 'person of experience'.

Gealla, derived from *geal*, meaning 'bright' and 'wild'. Lough Gill in County Sligo is named for her. (Female form of Lugh.)

Gealtraí, meaning happy music.

Goll Mac Morna was leader of the Fianna before Fionn.

Goltraí, meaning melancholic music.

Grannia, who eloped with Diarmait, was the daughter of Cormac mac Airt, high chieftain of Ireland.

Grianán is a summer or sun home.

Gulbain, a monstrous boar was born human but became enchanted when he was brought back to life after being killed by Donn, the god of darkness or death who crushed him between his knees at Tara in a fit of jealousy. He gave his name to Ben Gulbáin or Ben Bulben, a snout-shaped ben or mountain peak in north Sligo

Hy Brassil, the Isle of the Blest, was the Otherworld beyond the sea.

Imbolc, the festival to celebrate spring and the lactation of ewes.

Keash means 'wicker-work' and is a common name in Ireland for places where a wicker causeway is used to bridge a stream. It became a place name, as the small mountain in County Sligo, for a local object near the stream.

Kitchen Middens are shell dumps from sea-food harvesting.

Knock na Rae, Hill of the Moon, a prominent mountain in County Sligo.

Leath Ros, a headland of Sligo bay, the original name of Strand-hill.

Lia Fáil, the Stone of Destiny standing investiture stone at Tara.

Lios Tóghail, the election place, the investiture site at Carrowmore.

Lugh was the De Danaan god of genius and light. (Male form of Gealla.)

Lughnasa is the harvest festival of Lugh.

Lug na nGall, meaning the 'Rock of the Foreigners', is a prominent peak in the Benbulben range of mountains in County Sligo.

Maebh or Mebh, was the warrior chieftain of Connaght.

Maebh's Carn, a large carn on top of Knock na Rae.

Maigh Tuireadh, meaning the 'grassy plane of towers or tears or reckonings' is in County Sligo.

Midhe, or Meath, was the fifth and innermost province of Ireland.

Nás na Rí, in County Kildare was the hosting place of chieftains.

Nemeton, a space cleared around a pool or stream in a forest to attract game birds and animals. Later used as corrals or animal enclosures.

Niamh Cinn Óir, Niamh (pronounced Niev in English) of the Golden Hair, the fairy woman that stole the heart of Oisín, son of Fionn.

Nial Naoi nGiallioch, meaning 'Niall of the Nine Fosterings', was a high chieftain of Ireland around 405 AD.

Ogham, an early Irish form of writing named for Oghma, the ancient De Danaan god of wisdom or literature.

Oghamra, a romanised form of Oghma to conceal the original form.

Oisín, son of Fionn Mac Cumhal by Saba, the Fairy Doe.

Pooka, sneaky fairies that wander at night looking for mischief.

Romera, a romanised name to conceal the Daghda.

Ros, Rosses Point, a headland of Sligo bay.

Saba, the fairy doe wife of Fionn and mother of Oisín.

Samhrain, Halloween, the festival of autumn abundance.

Sidhe, a fairy hill or mound, carn or cave or seat of power.

Sligo, Sligeach or 'the Shelly Place', is a small city, population circa 25,000, in the north west of Ireland.

Suantraí, peaceful music.

Tara, Teamhair, an eminent place used as the centre of Irish De Danaan administration, was named for Tea, wife of a high chieftain.

Táin Bó Cuailgne, the Cattle raid of Cooley, a story of Maebh's challenge for acceptance as a valid high chieftain of Ireland.

Tír na n'Óg, the Land of Youth and Promise, the Otherworld.

Tory, an island off the Donegal coast, a place of pirates.

Triple Spiral, symbol of the three faces of the goddess.

Tuan, an ancient shape-changing story teller.

Tuatha Dé Danaan, the people of Danu from the Danube region.

Túr Connaill, meaning 'Connaill's tower', the original builder of the Glass or Ice Tower on Tory Island taken by Balor.

Uaimh na gCat, the Cave of the Cats, is at Crúacháin Ái in County Roscommon. From it came many plagues of cats, dogs and pigs to ravage Connaght.

Uisce Beatha, blessed water, from which derived the word 'whiskey'.

Well of Healing under Heapstown Carn in County Sligo. Covered by the Fomorians to stop the De Danaans from healing their wounded at the battle of Maigh Tuireadh.

Sligo Myths and Legends School

Guided Tours of:
Carrowmore, Knock na Rea, Fairy Glen.
Lough Gill and Its Islands, The Holy Well and Carn's Hill

Hear the Myths and Legends.
See what inspired the Druids, Bards and Poets.
Feel the excitement of ancient wisdom.
Know the mystery of an ancient people.
Feel the mystery of the three faces of the goddess:
The Lake, the River and the Sea.

Tours are lead by:
Michael, *Storyteller and Anthropologist*
Stephen, *Guide and Archaeologist*
Rebecca and Brian, *Storytellers and Actors*

The tour promotes interest in the narratives, rituals and history embedded in the Sligo landscape. Enthusiastic speakers will elaborate on the local and ancient narrative each morning and on selected sites each afternoon.

The tour typically runs for two days:
10.00 am to 4.30 pm each day:

Day 1: Carrowmore's panoramic landscape.

Day 2: Lough Gill, Holy Well and Carns Hill.

€75.00 per day.   Both days €120.00

Phone/text 087-1378077 or Email: info@lughzone.com

Visit our website at www.Lughzone.com